D0984442

FOREWORD BY POPPY Z. BRITE
ILLUSTRATIONS AND AFTERWORD
BY J. K. POTTER

GOLDEN GRYPHON PRESS • 2003

Louisiana
BREAKDOWN

LUCIUS SHEPARD

Copyright © 2003 by Lucius Shepard
Foreword copyright © 2003 by Poppy Z. Brite
Afterword copyright © 2003 by J. K. Potter
Illustrations copyright © 2003 by J. K. Potter

Edited by Marty Halpern

LIBRARY OF CONGRESS CATALOGUING-IN-PUBLICATION DATA
Shepard, Lucius.
    Louisiana breakdown / by Lucius Shepard ; with a foreword by
Poppy Z. Brite ; and an afterword and interior illustrations
by J. K. Potter. – 1st ed.
      p.   cm.
    ISBN 1-930846-14-2 (hardcover : alk. paper)
      1. Louisiana—Fiction.   2. Summer solstice—Fiction.
3. Festivals—Fiction.   4. Queens—Fiction.   I. Title.
PS3569.H3939 L68   2003
813'.54—dc21   2002014587

Printed in the United States of America.
First Edition

Contents

To Mark and Nancy Jacobson

Foreword

I AM NOT CERTAIN WHY I HAVE BEEN ASKED TO WRITE this introduction, since Lucius Shepard was publishing great stories like "Delta Sly Honey" in *Twilight Zone* when I was a pup with no credentials whatsoever. It's rather like Barry Whitwam, the drummer of Herman's Hermits, being asked to introduce this great new album *Rubber Soul*. You don't need me to hype Lucius to you, but since I'm here, I'll attempt to say a few semicogent things about *Louisiana Breakdown* before letting you get to it.

A local friend and I have recently been making fun of most fiction set in New Orleans and the rest of south Louisiana —two distinct environs frequently confused by writers who populate the French Quarter with Cajuns and drop Marie Laveau off somewhere near Lafayette. He e-mailed me about a day in the life of a typical New Orleans character: "Wake up in an unairconditioned, dimly lit room (or houseboat on 'the bayou,' wherever the fuck that is), light a cigarette, blow smoke into the ceiling fan and gripe to yourself about the stifling heat. . . ." I wrote back to describe a mystery novel I'd read in which the heroine fell off a wrought-iron balcony and landed in a giant king cake, and I concluded the e-mail, "Hang on, Boudreaux's at the door. We're going to the Mardi Gras parade. Hope he brought me a nice sack of crawfish."

You live in a fairy tale, you get bombarded with clichés. In south Louisiana, one of our pitiful defenses against this is to mock ourselves more readily and viciously than any outsider can, congratulating ourselves on the quaintness of our corrupt politicians and bragging about being the murder capital of America (I believe New Orleans earned that dubious distinction in 1993). As Miss Sedele Monroe, a character in *Louisiana Breakdown*, points out, "New York, Los Angeles . . . Omaha, you look beneath the surface, it's nuts everywhere. Difference 'tween the rest of the world and Grail, our surface been peeled away for a couple hundred years. We in what'cha might call plain fuckin' view."

Which just goes to show that another, better defense is to write honestly about the place, but that's difficult to do. I've been writing about it since 1986 and haven't acquitted myself yet. I usually tell people that John Kennedy Toole's *A Confederacy of Dunces* is the only honest book ever written about New Orleans. In truth, there's a handful of fiction that manages to plumb the region's magic without drowning in the clichés. *Louisiana Breakdown* is such a piece.

In particular, Lucius Shepard captures the south Louisiana sense of pantheism better than any other author I've read. The Native American gods became swamp monsters, the Catholic saints merged bloodily with the Creole voodoo pantheon, the Old Ones stopped by a storefront church on Claiborne Avenue, and we still pray to any and all of them according to what seems most efficacious. Some of these characters understand that, some are snared by it unsuspecting, but all are affected. Imagine this told in Lucius's lyrical-badass voice, like some hybrid of Orpheus and Tom Waits talking about "white ribbon tied around a cypress trunk" and "this chicory-flavored nowhere" and Vietnamese neon characters seen through mist, and you'll have *Louisiana Breakdown*. Go on now—and enjoy your vacation in Grail. You won't really understand it unless you're from there, but it will change you, and that is the most important thing we can ask of travel.

> Poppy Z. Brite
> New Orleans
> July 2002

Louisiana
Breakdown

1

June 22

*Y*OU EVER HEAR ABOUT THIS LITTLE PLACE DOWN IN Louisiana, this nowhere town on the Gulf name of Grail? Got a sugar refinery what's been shut down, waters are near fished out. Scrawny old suspender-wearing men listening to baseball on the gas station radio, spitting Red Man and staring at the license plates of cars that burn past without even slowing, on their way to somewhere better, though the old men wouldn't never admit it. Business district is a couple of blocks of Monroe Street. Shops in three-story buildings of friable brick that were new in turn-of-the-century photographs. Faded advertisements painted on the walls portraying sewing machines and refrigerators and shoes from the 1930s, the windows so dusty, God only knows what's sold inside. Dinged cars and battered pickups parked on the slant with gray patches of Bondo on their fenders, Ragin' Cajun decals polka-dotting the windshields. Bait store, grain store, convenience store, all faced with white plastic panels, and signs on the poles outside with misspelled words in black stick-on letters and prices with the numbers hanging cockeyed.

Fishing boats moored at a weathered pier that juts out into a notch of the Gulf, every metal surface scabbed with rust, grimy blue rag tied like a tourniquet around a broken mast.

Creosote smell from the pilings.

Brine and gasoline.

A pelican with spread wings perched on an oil drum.

There's enough bars to keep a town twice the size drunk forever, and more than enough drunks to keep them busy. Cross streets with aluminum-sided houses, some smaller than the tombs you find in St. Louis Number Two graveyard back in New Orleans. Elementary school named for a football player. The Assembly of God Church looks like a white army barracks and, separated from it by a neat green lawn, St. Jude's is a frame structure with a clapboard steeple that looks as if it should be New England Episcopal and not Roman Catholic. Churchgoers will pile out of the doors, mingle on the lawn, a syncretism of hellfire shouters and mystical animists. Florid men in plaid jackets, white belts, and pastel slacks talking real estate and golf with leaner men wearing Elvis Presley sideburns and black suits. Wives smile and clutch purses to their waists. Sunday thoughts slide like swaths of gingham through their minds.

Beyond the brick buildings, the businesses thin out along Monroe, weedy vacant lots between them, palmettos fountaining up, hibiscus bushes and a few scrub oaks, the ground littered with beer cans and condoms and yellowed newspapers.

Crosson's Hardware, where you can purchase any kind of firepower, lay bets, join the Klan.

Joe Dill Realty, Joe Dill Brokerage, Joe Dill Construction, all occupying the Dill Building, along with a dentist, a doctor, an accountant, the town ambulance chaser.

Police station, barbershop, Whitney Bank.

A boarded-up arcade, a little concrete box postage-stamped to infinity with posters and placards advertising revivals, carnivals, failed politicians.

Dairy Queen.

Nights, kids sit on stone benches out front, in the spill of glare from the cash window, sipping milk shakes, licking that soft ice cream with the curlicue on top, while others cruise in a tight circle around the building, gunning their engines, the radios up loud. Kids from Grail High, the Grail Crusaders. Basketball team made it to the state semis this year, and everybody was real proud. Watching from a distance, you have the idea that something more than what's apparent must be going on, that it's a Norman Rockwell nightmare. Like the kids are programmed by some hellish force, they're speaking Latin backwards, they're on the lookout for enemies of Satan. Black silhouettes shading their eyes against headlights, peering to see who's riding in the cars. A couple starts dancing to heavy metal on a boom box. Moths whirling above their heads are the souls of the damned.

Police cruiser idles, rumbling on the corner opposite, a ruby cigarette coal glowing behind the windshield.

Screams, wild laughter, glass breaking.

Two shadows stepping fast past Louisianne Hair Boutique, Dill's Liquors, Jolly's Lumber.

In the window of Cutler's Lawn and Garden there's a huge poster showing shiny red tractors and green cultivators and yellow riding mowers trundling over a section of perfect farmland, like an opening into a better world.

THIS IS JOHN DEERE COUNTRY reads the banner above it.

The Gulfview Motel is six pink stucco cabins with peaked roofs and a plaster birdbath next to the office. Across the street, Club Le Bon Chance, a low concrete block building with electric Dixie Beer ads tattooing the black windows, and a neon sign shaped like a pair of dice that tumble a ways over the rooftop and change from showing a four and a three to snake eyes. The parking lot's never empty, the music never ends. Miss Sedele Monroe grows older at the end barstool every day from two P.M. until something intriguing comes along, soothing her redheaded soul with mysterious elixirs. Her life's a scarlet rumor. They say you ain't lived 'til she's doctored your Charlie, but just don't go and let that green left eye of hers lock onto yours.

Presley's original drummer, D. J. Fontana, plays at the club now and then. Talks about barnstorming through Louisiana in a pink Cadillac. How the women were, how the rednecks wanted to cut them. People come from all over, stare at him like he's a holy relic. He's so old, they say with fond, delicate amazement. He's so old.

Two men killed recently, one knifed beside the pool table, the other beaten to death in the john.

Charlotte Slidell of Golden Harvest, 23, was last seen dancing there one April night two years ago.

This time of year, it always seems hotter after dark.

Sunsets are terrific here. There's no work to be had, but patriotism runs high. They say it's a great place to raise kids. Solid values, clean air. The kids can't wait to leave. You might wonder why anyone would want to stay in a place like this, a place that has about as much purpose as a fly buzzing around something that ain't fit to eat. What keeps them going year after year through boredom and welfare hassles, hurricanes and heat? Belief, that's the answer. Not belief in God necessarily, nor in America. Nothing that simple. These people have a talent for belief. They've learned to believe in whatever's necessary to preserve the illusion of the moment. They'll tell you stories about the Swamp Child, about the Kingdom of the Good Gray Man, about voodoo and hoodoo and how you can do it to whoever you want long as you got the coin to pay the old Nanigo woman who lives in the mangrove where mosquitoes whine and gators belly-flop into the black water. Jesus Lives. So does Shango, Erzulie, Damballa, half a dozen others. Plastic Virgin tacked to a wall, with paper hearts and broken scissors and a wristband of goat hair on the altar beneath. White ribbon tied around a cypress trunk. One hundred red candles burning on a porch. The believers softly breathe. Whisper the words. They smile, they nod. The mystic is here. Ineffable voices are heard. The anonymous saints of endurance manifest. This is the one true home.

They don't care if you believe it. They know, they know. Strangers can't understand the secrets they control.

Miss Nedra Hawes, Oracles and Psychic Divination.

Crescents and ankhs and seven-pointed stars.

With a noise like birdshot ripping through leaves, a sudden gust drives grit against the windows of Vida's Moonlight Diner, a railroad car painted white and decorated all over with groupings of brightly colored lines. *Veves.* Voodoo sign.

Past the diner, on the eastern edge of town, a dirt road lined with shotgun cabins leads off toward the Gulf. Shotgun Row. That's where the blacks live, some poor whites, other outcasts, the cabins blended in with cypress, live oaks, swamp. Past the dirt road, past the city limits and the dump, past the winding asphalt road that leads to the development where most of the solid citizens live, there's a trail barely noticeable from the highway. A footpath choked by chicory bushes, wild indigo, ferns. No one ever goes there, no offerings are left to appease or placate. Children are not warned away. It's not evil, it's simply a forgotten place, or else a place people want to forget. Standing there, watching grackles hopping in the high branches of an oak, slants of paling dust-hung light touching the tops of the bushes, listening to chirrs and p'weets and frogs ratcheting, you get the feeling that something's living out in the shadows, out with the two-headed lizards and the albino frogs, all the mutant things of pollution, something big and heavy and slow and sad, not a threat to anything but itself, something that wanders through the green shade, lost and muttering, peeking between the leaves, ducking whenever a car passes, scurrying back to its hole. There's a secret here, a powerful secret. An old tension in the air. But who controls it, who does it control? That's a secret nobody wants to know.

Ribbon of dark water veining into the swamp beyond.

Wind makes a river, the trees make a moan.

Spider web trembles, but the spider ain't home. Moonlight slips like a silver fluid down the strands, the whole structure belling, the strange silky skeleton woven of a life through time, fragile yet resilient for all its frays, beautiful despite the husks of recent victims and the unconsumed legs of a dead lover.

The baseball game has ended. The old men are tucking their tobacco pouches away, getting ready to go home. One slaps the radio in disgust. It takes some of them two, three tries to heave up from their chairs. Down at the pier, Joe Dill, a muscular black-haired man in jeans and a blue work shirt steps from the cabin of a fishing boat, flings down a wrench and looking up, says "Shit!" to the sky. The parking lot behind the Dill Building is emptying, the cars heading east out of town, some pulling into Club Le Bon Chance. A string of pelicans crosses the breakwater, flapping, then gliding, spelling out a sentence of cryptic black syllables against the overcast. A crane steps with Egyptian poise through scummy shallows. Sandpipers scuttle along a ragged strip of tawny beach west of the pier. Potbellied, their heads tipped back, they stop and pose like pompous little professors. Candy-flake red Camaro Z–28 lays rubber down Monroe, and a bald man who's locking up a shop in one of the brick buildings scowls and shakes his head. A frail, wrinkled lady in a lace-collared dress tapping with her cane along the sidewalk, heading back from Dill's Liquors, her shopping bag heavy with a week's supply of vodka. Two teenage girls sneaking a joint in the alley between the arcade and the bank watch her pass with somber expressions, and once she's out of sight they exchange glances and break out in giggles.

Somewhere a chained-up dog is barking crazy.

The years spin and divide, flaking into days. The days run off like rain down a window.

It's coming on twilight now.

2
June 22 – 6:66 P.M.

*A*NOTHER MUGGY EVENING, THE ASS-END OF ANOTHER worthless day. Standing on her cabin porch, Vida Dumars watched the Great Cloud of Being drift in off the Gulf to shadow the town. She recognized it by the Nine Forms, which were wisping up and dissolving in the frays at its edges. The one other time the Cloud had appeared, eleven years back when she was just eighteen, she had run away from Grail to be a wild child in New Orleans, to live with the witch man, Clifford Marsh, and so she took this new apparition for a sign that her life was about to undergo a change. That frightened Vida. Change was the last thing she wanted, especially if it led to the sort of abuse she'd suffered with Marsh. She would have liked to shut the cabin door and make believe the Cloud had gone away. But that would have been purely ignorant, and although Vida was distracted for sure and crazy maybe, she had left ignorance behind when she had run back to Grail. She studied the Cloud's bumpy underside, hunting for a clue that might tell her something about the change to come. Grumbling overhead. Splotch of tin-

9

colored light shining through the overcast in the west. But no real clues. After almost an hour, sluggish with dread and depression, she went inside to fix her supper.

The Cloud eventually moved off to the northeast, dragging in behind a sheet of darkness and stars. Vida struck out through the brush behind the cabin, keeping to a worn path that meandered among scrub palmetto, acacias, and stands of bamboo, heading for Thalia's Pond and a swim. The pond was shaded by massive live oaks, crowded round by thickets, the banks edged by swamp cabbage and flowering weeds. Darkness welled from gaps between the trees. Stillness of cicadas and frogs, whispers of wind. A sheen of starlight polished the water. When she dove in, she had the notion she had slit a seam in some strangely permeable black mineral and that it had closed without a ripple over her, becoming black stone. It always surprised her that she could surface. When she shook her long chestnut hair, diamonds sprayed from the wet ends. The cool water tingled with the still-alive atoms of the demon that had been dissolved there a century ago by a Nanigo witch. Vida wondered if he could feel her, if he could know pleasure from her. Sometimes, the way the water gloved her, tighter and slicker than the Gulf water, she was certain that he could. Sometimes just going with that thought gave her the pleasure of a man.

She swam under the newly risen moon, which looked like pieces of a busted silver mirror that someone had tacked up among the leaves. Her thoughts came in pictures, and she floated among them, conjuring up old friends. Once they had seemed embodiments of her need. Complex accessories to her joy. Now they had for her the simplicity of ancient statues, abandoned and isolate mysteries like cemetery figures wrapped in vines of circumstance, their marble streaked with burned-out veins of sick desire. But she still saw herself the way she had when she was young. Damaged some, and confused plenty, yet still clear and needful, an appetite with blood and breasts and tongue. She half-believed that time was running slow for her and fast for everybody else, hauling her

along through the limbo it created in its wake, steeping her in
the shade and not the bright center of life, and she didn't
know whether that was bad or good. Thinking like this heav-
ied her, disturbed the engines of her equilibrium. She had to
swim to keep afloat, stroking back and forth across the pond
with the metronomic persistence of a wind-up toy. Toning the
heart, the long, smooth muscles. She felt she was tunneling,
catching a handful of the black water and throwing it behind,
herself forward. Back and forth. Touching the bank and turning. Just getting up to speed before she had to turn again.
Light splintering in her eyes.

When she was done swimming she stretched out on a flat
rock at the south end of the pond to dry. The moon licked at
her with its cool tongue, a weed nodded and tickled her
thigh. She was tall and long-legged, a couple of inches under
six feet, with a trim waist and flaring hips and pale freckly skin
that made you think of the shells of farm eggs, the dusting
heaviest across the slopes of her breasts. The kind of body
guys would stare at slack-jawed from cars trembling at stop-
lights, and say to their buddies, lookit there, I'd like to get me
some of that, and then shout some madness about pussy and
drive away fast. Her features were strong—too strong, her
detractors would say, to be called beautiful—and the irises
of her dark brown eyes showed clean as targets against the
whites. There was something daunting about the statuesque
perfection of her body and the masklike stoicism of her
features. It was as if she embodied an ideal of beauty, not
beauty's delicate particularity and warmth. Marsh had called
her The Princess—it was not a term of endearment, but one
calculated to distinguish her from the rest of his coterie, to
give measure to the fact that when most anyone looked at her,
they perceived her to be imperious and cold. That Vida sure
is took with herself, they'd say, she sure is one stuck-up bitch.
And yet they also had a sneaking suspicion that she was too
good for them, that fate had marked her for special usage.
They could love her and hate her in the same breath, and
were so put off by the impression of strength and calm they

received back from her, they only realized in retrospect that she was beautiful. But that impression was entirely misleading. Vida was far more beautiful than she was strong. She'd used up much of her strength in tearing herself away from Marsh. At the best of times she was skittish, prone to anxiety attacks, and each night she was tormented by dreams. She believed that through them Marsh was forcing her to live out the years as they might have been had she stayed in New Orleans to endure his usage. Her life had become a process of holding out against those dreams, and it was getting to be a harder struggle every day.

Once she was dry she gathered her clothes and set out for home, not bothering to dress, liking the feel of the warm air on her skin. Thalia's Pond had a bad reputation. Nobody strayed there after dark . . . except the Guidry children, whose entire family ran around buck-naked themselves. She figured it wouldn't be much cause for titillation if they had a peek. The swim had washed away her gloom, and the sizzling of crickets and cicadas gladdened her. As did the feathery gestures of the palmettos, the shadowy gateways of the bamboo. But as she reached a bend in the path, she began to have a sense that the moon, bobbling along to the rhythm of her footsteps above the tree line, was actually following her. She let out a laugh, trying to deny the feeling, but the shakiness of the laugh dismayed her. She picked up the pace. Palmettos bristled in a wind that kicked up of a sudden; the acacias leaned down toward her, and the blue-black starry sky lowered with the ponderous slowness of a collapsing circus tent. As if the night had suddenly changed its character, as if it had become angry at her intrusion into secret places. A queasy chill uncoiled in her belly. Felt like spiders traipsing up her backbone. She twitched her head from side to side. To the north, atop a low hill, a dead water oak with knobbly arms and forked-twig hands seemed to spring from nowhere and brand its witchy shape onto her brain. Marsh, she said to herself, it's Marsh. But then she thought, no, it's just wind, just nerves. She walked faster yet, pretending to ignore the slithers and whisperings. The bushes were talking about her, telling evil lies. Off to the left, a rustle. Something moving parallel to the path. She started to run, her breath shrieking. Clothes spilled from her arms. Bushes lashed her breasts, her arms; roots humped up to snag her ankles. Something, a bug maybe, buzzed past her ear, caught in her hair, and that panicked her worse than anything. She pictured a tiny winged devil burrowing through the damp tangles, getting ready to bore into her skull and breed. She tore at her scalp, raked her hair, wanting to snatch it out. She staggered off-balance and sprawled flat on her stomach right where the path widened into a sandy oval clearing picketed by bamboo.

She rolled over, a scream caged in her throat, certain that something monstrous would break from the thickets. Nothing, nothing, nothing. Moon-lacquered yellow stalks and sprig leaves hanging limp. The wind had died, the rustling had stopped. The clearing appeared to have closed in around her. Bamboo shadows slanted over hummocky sand and grass. The stillness frightened her as much as the tumult. If she moved a muscle, the wind and the rustling would come again. She lay propped on her elbows, knees partway drawn up, waiting for a sign that it would be all right to scramble to her feet and run, that the night had forgiven her. Then one of the bamboo shadows directly in front of her began to grow long. Inch by inch, it stretched out across the ground. She watched with the horrified fascination of someone mesmerized by a cobra rising from a basket. She refused to believe it at first. It was too much like her dreams. Yet there it was. Creeping inch by inch. A black pipe of shadow aimed straight between her legs. She saw the king stalk of bamboo, a glowing golden tube rising from the picket line, elongating and fattening. The brighter it shined, the blacker the shadow. She knew what was going to happen and her fear burned so fiercely, she thought she could manage to stand. But that was an illusion. Her strength fled, her will sheared away. She couldn't turn her head or blink, only watch and tremble. Her mind was a stone and her thought a vein of hot color twisting through it. The bamboo shadow grew longer, its end vanishing in the shadow of her knees. Then it touched. Hesitated. The touch, the tension it brought, made her feel that her skull had been poured brimful of a fuming liquid and it was about to boil over. In reflex, her hips betrayed her and nudged forward. Fear was so intense now, so pure an anticipation, it was the same as pleasure. Then the shadow penetrated, going in slow at first. And then it plunged deep. Cold . . . God, it was cold. Heavy and hurtful like cold iron, working to get its whole length in, settling and holding for a second just like a man. Cold killed the sounds, palsied her limbs. Impaled, she fell backward, clawing up handfuls of sand. Her hips were lifted, and the cold spread through her, making her thrust and give. The shadow rammed in and out, churning her hips. Something was breaking inside her, and she thought, It's killing me. She was almost grateful—it was too hard to live. But soon she realized that the breaking thing wasn't death. Waves of breakage pushed up from her center, from a place no one had touched for so long . . . not since Marsh. And that was the cruelest hurt, to know that he could have her yet, that she was still twisting on his pivot. She caught sight of the moon. Faceless, eyeless. But it saw her, it was part of this. And the trees, too. They were crying out, mimicking delight. She bit her lip hard to keep from joining their chorus. Each wave flung her high, then dragged her back below the horizon of consciousness, from dazzled light into blackness and burning. The sky completed its collapse, the stars were fireflies shining in her hair. Sand grains pricked her ass, grass blades stuck to her thighs. The world tipped sideways. She was cresting the last wave, pouring off the edge. She fought it, but the wave was too powerful. God. The black sun. The fall. Seizures of joy, spasms. The most you can hope for in Hell. Blood flowing out around a stalk of shadow. She was for a moment perfected, poised between things and the uncreate, held up to light and dark, an offering. And then she was gasping, abandoned, stranded in a place whose name and particulars she couldn't remember. Trickles of sand sifted through her unclenching fingers.

She sat up after awhile.

Everything looked scattered, as if before there had been a unity. A patternless chaos of weeds and bird droppings and flattened beer cans. The bamboo had pulled back from the clearing. Shadows were not so sharp, and the moon was an empty power.

Damn fool, her. Going swimming in the devil's flesh so close to St. John's Eve.

Marsh, she thought, working up fresh hate for him, afraid that she wouldn't be able to believe he had been to blame, that she would continue to blame herself. She said his name, said it again and again until it was like she was spitting out black seeds of him.

"Please," she said. "Please . . . somebody help me." And hated herself for that weakness. He was subtle, he never left her anything to hang onto, he wanted her to doubt herself. She felt like crying, but she refused to give in to the urge. She was cold. Not like before, but cold enough.

Finally she got to her feet and went back along the path, picking up her clothes. She pulled on her jeans and her plaid shirt, crumpled up her panties into a ball. She toe-and-heeled into her sneakers. Still cold. She cocked an ear, listening to the frogs, the cicadas. The slop of the Gulf water was audible now the wind had died. It seemed she knew something more than she had, that secret knowledge had come to her. But when she tried to fix on it, there was only the usual. Vida Dumars has a past, owns a diner and lives alone, a mystery to everyone she meets. That was the sum of her. The balled-up lump of years, with dirt impacting the folds. She needed secret knowledge, something to help her spin away from Marsh's hold. Salvation maybe, a fit thrown down in front of a gawping congregation, a hole blasted through into her brain to let the balm of God flow in. No troubles anymore once you let Jesus take control. Something. Miss Sedele down at Le Bon Chance had her own ideas as to what that something should be, but though she done worse than lie down with another woman, Vida wasn't ready to grasp at that particular straw.

The wind sprang up again, hissing in the palmetto fronds, stirring the bamboo, vibrating the shadows. It seemed to amplify the jittering of the stars. Strands of Vida's hair, dry now, feathered across her face. Her cheeks were flushed, and the skin between her shoulder blades prickled. The branches of her being sprouted new sensitive buds, picking up sly movements here and there. She had a look behind her, to the side, and hurried toward the cabin.

What the hell had she been doing? Just standing around and feeling the breeze, acting like nothing had happened?

After a bit she slowed down, started watching where she was going. She didn't want to be alone tonight; she needed people around her, even if they were only the freaks and losers who swung their partners over at Le Bon Chance. Marsh wouldn't make her suffer anymore. Not just yet. She belonged to him and he enjoyed the fact of her belonging too much to push her off the edge. In his own way, he was temperate.

For this one night, at least, their affair was over.

3

June 22 – 9:11 P.M.

*M*USTAINE WAITED FOR THE TOW TRUCK BENEATH the sign that presided over the outskirts of Grail. It was, he thought, a truly weird sign, smacking of a wry self-regard that seemed out of character for rural Louisiana. It was mounted on metal poles that elevated it above buzzing thickets at the side of the road, thirty feet or so from the shoulder where his red BMW was parked. A rectangle about the size of a double bed, lit by a sputtering fluorescent tube that flared as bright as a bar of burning magnesium. Swarms of moths fluttered around it, like shadows of leaves scattered by a wind nobody could feel. *WELCOME TO GRAIL . . . LOUISIANA PURE AND SIMPLE* was painted in script across the top, and occupying the remainder of the space was the line rendering of a chalice similar to those used to serve communion wine—Mustaine had supposed that a grail was intended. On second glance, though, he realized the lines might just as easily be seen to portray two identical human profiles staring at one another; depending on how you focused, you could see either the cup or the profiles, as with that old psychological test for evaluating perceptual bias.

Headlights coming from the direction of town. The tow truck, maybe. He wondered what kind of place Grail was. Odds were he'd have time to find out. It wasn't likely they'd have parts for a BMW. A mosquito buzzed him, whined in his ear. He gave it a half-hearted slap. Sweat trickled down the back of his neck. The humid air clotted like glue in his throat. He considered the sign. What had it meant that he'd seen the chalice first? Maybe he'd failed the test. Can't stay the night in Grail, son, 'less you see the two faces. He laughed. It probably meant he needed a couple of drinks. The headlights veered toward him, blinding, and he shielded his eyes, trying to see the car. Lights bracketed to a white roof. Police. He'd smoked the last of his dope back in Texas, but he was nervous nonetheless. A shadow climbed from the cop car, leaving the engine idling, and moseyed over. The beam from a flashlight speared into Mustaine's eyes.

"Evening, officer," he said. "I'm just waiting for a tow."

The cop was young, maybe younger than Mustaine, but taller, wider, with a mean cracker face and a bad pimple . beside his nose; he wore a sorrowful, dyspeptic look.

"Whyn't you get up some ID," he said.

Mustaine fished out his wallet. "You didn't see a tow truck heading this way, didja? Man stopped earlier, said he'd send out a tow truck."

The cop took Mustaine's driver's license, shined his flashlight on it; the webbed lines on his knuckles were etched deep with grime. "This ain't you," he said after a significant pause.

The photograph showed Mustaine with black hair down past his shoulders, his long face fuller, his blue eyes cored with glowing red dots from the flash. It was a photograph of manic excess, of a devout delusionary. Looking at it, he felt dislocated, off-balance, as if affected by a slight diminution of gravity—the way it goes when you gaze through the wrong end of a telescope at something close to hand.

"I got a haircut," he said. "Lost some weight."

"When you born?" The cop moved the license so Mustaine couldn't peek.

"August 21, 1969. Deland, Florida."

Mustaine rested his hand on the BMW's hood and jerked it away. Still too hot to touch. Everything was hot. The air, the frying noises of crickets, the feeling in his head. Even the moon hanging over the Gulf, almost full, like a melted spotlight. Maybe this is justice, he thought, maybe justice feels this way. Like hot static and stuck somewhere in the middle of the dark with a big ugly fucker who's got nothing better to do.

A car cruised toward them, slowed. The cop waved, a honk, and then the car—a black Corvette—accelerated, exceeding the speed limit.

"Man's in a hurry," said Mustaine, hoping the cop might notice and give chase.

"Wouldn't worry 'bout him if I's you." The cop studied the license a while longer before handing it back; he squinted at Mustaine. " 'Pears yo' barber didn't stand close enough to you."

Fuck you, Mustaine thought, and was tempted to ask if they still hated hippies here. Was Vietnam still an issue?

A vehicle with a winking caution light atop the roof pulled off onto the shoulder twenty yards away. Tow truck. Mustaine got the picture. Somebody had notified the wrecking service, told them that some guy with a fancy car and California plates was stalled east of town, and in the spirit of opportunism—like how about we screw a few bucks outa this fool?—the operator had called the cops. Looking away in frustration, Mustaine glanced up at the sign and this time saw the two faces; in the blue darkness above it the stars were thick and patternless.

The driver of the tow truck approached, taking a stand just beyond the spill of light from the sign; the cop sidled around back of the car, shined his flashlight in the window.

"What's all this heah?" he asked, indicating three guitar cases.

"Guitars," Mustaine said, his paranoia increasing.

"Open 'em up."

Mustaine pulled the cases out, set them on the hood and undid the latches. Inside were a Gibson L–5 with a cherry sunburst finish, an old white Telecaster, and a big blond Guild acoustic.

"You a musician?"

"That's right."

"My kid brother's got hisself a little group plays 'round heah."

"Oh, yeah?" Mustaine affected interest. "What's he play?"

"Buncha fuckin' noise makes him think he's God." The cop snorted in disgust. He plucked the B string of the Guild. "I s'pose you got bills of sale for these instruments."

Mustaine fought to keep irritation out of his voice. "I've had 'em for ten, fifteen years. Nobody keeps sales slips that long."

"These heah look pretty damn valuable. Somethin' valuable, you be wise to hang onto proof of ownership."

"The stores where I bought 'em'll have records."

"I s'pect so, but you might could do some real unpleasant waitin' if they take theah time sendin' 'em along." The cop held out his hand. "Lemme have yo' keys."

"Look," said Mustaine. "They're my guitars, okay? If you let me make a couple of calls . . ."

"Didn't say they wasn't yours." The cop waggled his fingers. "Keys."

After Mustaine had passed him the key ring, the cop tossed it to the driver and said, "Run it on in now, Wallace." Then he pointed to the cases. "Close 'em up. You kin stick 'em in the cruiser."

As he went about latching the cases, fetching them over to the police car, stowing them in the back seat, Mustaine toyed with the idea of making a break. It would be unrealistic to expect that he could escape, but the way things were shaping up he didn't much care for his chances no matter how you sliced it. They had his car, his guitars. Lot of money there. What was to stop them from dropping him into a bayou and chopping the BMW into spare parts? Selling the instruments, or maybe giving them as presents to brothers and nephews. He stood by the open rear door, beginning to shake with adrenaline, poised to run. He wiped sweat from his eyes.

"Go on . . . git in," said the cop.

A westbound car slowed. The black Corvette returning, its engine rumbling fatly, light channeled into shimmers along its hood. It pulled off the highway behind the BMW; its headlights drained shadows from ruts in the dirt shoulder. The cop said, "Goddamn it!" as a black-haired man in jeans and a blue work shirt climbed out and walked up to them. An Asian woman wearing a red *ao dai*, carrying a bottle of vodka, got out from the passenger side and leaned against the flank of the BMW. The man nodded pleasantly to Mustaine and said to the cop, "What's the story, Randy? You'n Wallace back in the rip-off business?" His voice, a baritone, was a couple of sizes too big for his body, but had no real richness or tonality; it was simply big and peremptory, falsely emotive in the way of an actor who was just learning to project.

"You got no call stickin' yo' nose in," said the cop.

"I was waiting for a tow," Mustaine said eagerly, staking his hopes on this stranger. "I don't know what the hell's going on."

The man hitched his thumbs in his hip pockets and regarded the cop with displeasure. He was short and heavily muscled, his hair a cap of tight curls that fit low on his forehead. His face was tanned, deeply lined, but the lines betrayed neither gloom nor meanness nor good humor; they appeared to be incidental detail. His features were generous, yet unremarkable. He resembled, Mustaine thought, a police sketch that had captured the likeness—but not the character—of a handsome Italian suspect.

"This boy's got valuable musical instruments," the cop said, pointing out the guitar cases. "He ain't got shit to prove he owns 'em."

"Lemme see if I got this straight," said the man. "You're bustin' him 'cause he's got a coupla guitars?"

The Asian woman laughed and had a sip of the vodka. She

had a sexy catlike face, with full lips and almond eyes. Her nipples poked up the silk of the *ao dai*; black hair tumbled about her shoulders. She caught Mustaine staring and laughed again.

"What am I s'posed to do with you, Randy?" the man said to the cop in a tone of patience sorely tried. "I told you I won't tolerate this shit." He looked to the tow truck driver. "Put this man's possessions back in his car. And send me the bill for the repairs."

The driver said he'd take care of it and started hauling the guitar cases; the cop scowled and adjusted the hang of his holster.

"Now look heah, Joe," he said. "I know you 'spect people to squawk ever' time you set on a tack, but you can't go 'round interferin' in police business."

"That is pretty bull-headed of me, isn't it?" said the man.

Mustaine sensed the possibility of violence. There was a passive menace about the man, a blankness, an absence of vibrations that was more unnerving than rage or any strong emotion would have been.

"I don't know 'bout 'bull-headed,' " said the cop, conciliatory now that he believed he had won a point. "God knows you got the right to have yo' say. But theah's a—"

The man planted a hand flat on the cop's chest. Mustaine expected him to shove the cop, but he just kept the hand there as if he were holding him up. The cop's Adam's apple bobbed; his eyes rolled down toward the hand. All the fizz had gone out of him. Mustaine could understand his reaction; he imagined how the hand felt—solid, a stony constraint, the frail heart beating against it, starting to ache, the skin growing painfully sensitive.

"Go away," said the man quietly. "Don't lemme see you 'round for awhile."

The cop stared at a point above the man's head; judging by the bewilderment of his expression, he might have been trying to recall something of profound importance.

"I'm not givin' you an option," said the man. "There's really nothin' to decide."

After a moment the cop swung on his heel and walked briskly back to the cruiser. A few seconds later he pulled the car into a tight U-turn and headed toward town.

"Stupid motherfucker!" The man spat out a breath, shook his head.

Mustaine realized that his own chest was aching. He let out a sigh to clear the feeling of constriction. The man was watching him with amusement.

"Thanks," Mustaine said. "I . . . uh . . ."

"No need," said the man. "It was begging to be done." He offered his hand; his grip was perfunctory, a quick squeeze. "My name's Joe Dill."

"Jack Mustaine."

"You're French extraction, are ya?" Joe Dill asked.

"Uh-huh."

"Me—" Joe Dill tapped his chest "—I'm Sicilian. The original name was Dilagrima, but my grandfather shortened it." He grinned. "I don't s'pose the old guy was aware of the humorous associations."

The driver of the tow truck began hooking up the BMW to his winch.

"So." Joe Dill rubbed his hands together. "How 'bout a drink? Lemme give you a proper welcome to Grail."

Mustaine was wary of this largesse, but Joe Dill steered him toward the Corvette. "I can't let people get this kinda impression of my town," he said. "It's a matter of upholdin' civic pride."

"I appreciate it." Mustaine slid into the passenger seat. "But I'm wiped out. I maybe should take a rain check."

"Just one drink. Then we'll find you a room."

To Mustaine's surprise the Asian woman eased in to sit on his lap, enveloping him in a scent of jasmine. She smiled at him over her shoulder, then applied a squirming pressure with her buttocks that kindled warmth in his groin.

"Pleased to meetcha," Mustaine said, wanting to present an unruffled front; he had an idea she would enjoy seeing him flustered.

"Okay, GI," said the woman, and giggled.

"You familiar with the Vietnamese?" asked Joe Dill, slipping behind the wheel, giving the woman's thigh a pat.

"I've known a couple," said Mustaine.

"They're an exceptional people. Truly exceptional."

"You were in Vietnam?" Mustaine asked.

Annoyance surfaced in Joe Dill's face. "No, I missed it." He nodded soberly as if agreeing with himself, then winked at Mustaine. "But I'm making up for it now."

The whimsical brightness with which he injected the statement unsettled Mustaine; he decided not to pursue the subject.

"You'll have to come visit me," said Joe Dill. "You'll see what I'm talkin' about." He glanced over at Mustaine. "I'm serious. You'd get a kick out of it. Maybe tomorrow, huh? But make it in the mornin'. From noon on I'll be busy with St. John's Eve." He must have noticed Mustaine's perplexity, because he said, "Most folks call it Midsummer Night's Eve. It's a big day for us. Quite a celebration. You picked a good night to have a breakdown."

Mustaine said that he'd have to see about his car, but maybe, yeah. With Joe Dill's aggressive and unwarranted friendliness, and the woman on his lap impeding movement, blocking his view, he was beginning to feel more imperiled than he had alone with the cop.

"Tuyet's Vietnamese," Joe Dill said.

"I figured."

"Yeah—" Joe Dill fired up the engine, gunned it "—'bout ten years back some shrimpers was givin' her family trouble over in Salt Harvest. I helped 'em out. Now she's helpin' me."

"Joe Dill number one American," said Tuyet.

Joe Dill grunted. "Don't let her fool you with that pidgin talk. She gotta degree from Sarah Lawrence."

As he peeled out, fishtailing into the wrong lane, Tuyet took the opportunity to give Mustaine's groin another massage. He had a glimpse of the gleaming white sign and its storm of moths. Once you noticed the profiles, it became difficult to see the grail. He supposed there was a lesson to be had from that—how a fascination with the superficial com-promised one's instinctive knowledge of the essential. The speed of the Corvette, the uncertainty of the situation, was making him feel young and uncaring. It occurred to him that this was the sort of feeling he had left Florida to recapture—to be lost and a little out of control, moving fast enough so that all the world became streaky lights, streaky darks.

"How you doin' there?" Joe Dill called out over the rush of the wind.

"Real great!" said Mustaine.

They rounded a curve, and as if the car were a compass needle oriented toward true north, the dome of the starry sky appeared to revolve a half-turn. The moon leaped along after them through the treetops like a bright monkey swinging branch to branch. The wind snuffed out the flame of Mustaine's paranoia and he began to anticipate the night ahead.

"Where we going?" he asked, clamping his hands to Tuyet's waist to keep her still.

Joe Dill, downshifting, said, "Little place up the road. You gonna love it," and once again Tuyet laughed.

4

June 22 — 11:07 P. M.

*7*HE JUKEBOX AT THE REAR OF LE BON CHANCE looked like the Crown of Creation, like a rococo neon cathedral on the fritz. It was the gaudiest jukebox Mustaine had ever seen. Big as a pop machine, nearly six feet of glowing purple and crimson plastic, with gold filigree worked into clawed feet, and blinking lights that sprayed beams of ruby and indigo into the dimness, and a pearly tubular arch framing the domed upper portion. He pictured it seven stories tall on a hill of cloud with an endless file of sinners stretching away from its base — the One True Jukebox, the jukebox in whose image all lesser jukeboxes had been created, validating the Victorian concept of the Great Good Time to be had beyond the threshold of a sober, dutiful life. Zydeco music honked from the speakers. People dancing in front of it were sainted with a radiant nimbus. To Mustaine, more than a little drunk, its glowing niche provided a safe harbor in which he could get his bearings and avoid further conversation with Joe Dill and Tuyet — she had been riding him ever since he had restrained her in the Corvette, and his temper had begun to fray. They were rolling poker dice at the bar with the owner of the club, Miss Sedele, a slim fortyish redhead in a lime-green cocktail dress, while one of the bartenders, a cadaverous man with a greasy black pompadour, offered commentary.

The room was about twice as long as it was wide. Hardwood floors and paneled walls on which were mounted photographs whose subject matter was hidden beneath glazes of reflection. Light bulbs in kerosene lamps hung from the ceiling cast a grainy yellowish murk. To the right of the jukebox was a bandstand, empty of equipment except for a solitary amp and a microphone, with stars and dice and smiling mouths of silver glitter pasted on the wall behind. To the left was a Ski Ball game; gathered around it, some old men were sucking on bottles of beer, watching younger men play. At the pool table a gawky kid with a prominent Adam's apple and a chinless inbred look was rolling a cue ball back and forth and watching flies circle. About a dozen couples—most in jeans —whirled and stomped to the Zydeco tune, and at the tables beyond the dance floor, between eighty and a hundred people were hooting, laughing, and waving their arms. Waitresses in shorts and tube tops and dice-shaped earrings weaved among them, slapping at groping hands, beer slopping everywhere. The feeling was of All American stupidity, of gleeful dullness and working class fury—a zooful of brown passions. But the bar itself seemed part of a quieter, more exotic dimension. A number of heavily made-up women in low-cut dresses sitting together at one end, sipping on drinks loaded with fruit and looking restless. Their eyes swiveled toward the door whenever it opened, and one was engaged in what might have been a negotiation with an old man in a pink jacket and plaid pants. Farther along, a female dwarf in patched overalls was chatting up a black man in a dark blue silk suit, his fingers aglint with gold and diamonds. Next to them eight very tall college-age men in suits and ties were nursing their beers; they appeared unsure, apprehensive. Also an enormous bearded man with the build of a professional wrestler, a long-haired boy with a silver metal guitar, and a

couple of girls who displayed the combination of studied
disinterest and couturier clothing that Mustaine associated
with big-time groupies. Then Joe Dill, Tuyet, and Miss
Sedele. Taking it all in, Mustaine wondered if every element
of Grail was imbued with this oddly congruent dissonance,
whether—if he cut with a scalpel, slicing off a section of the
entire town—he would find proportionate quantities of the
predictable and the unexpected in every cell.

He turned the jukebox's metal pages. There were familiar
names in among the Cajun and Zydeco tunes—Springsteen,
Randy Travis, Alabama—but the selections on several pages
were not only unfamiliar, they seemed once again to express
Grail's eccentric nature. The labels were not printed but
handwritten in a spidery script, and Mustaine had never
heard of any of the songs or artists; he doubted he would ever
have heard of them somewhere other than Grail, because the
titles and the artists' names had an idiosyncratic flair that
hinted at a homegrown perversity. AA–108, for instance, was
"Cruisin' For A Bruisin' " by Some Guys In The Blue Ford.
AA–112 was "Charlotte's Last Dance" by Person Or Persons
Unknown. BB–139 was "I Didn't Know She Was Married" by
The Salesman. Other titles were "Blast From The Past" by
Cody's Ex, "Satan Ain't Waitin' " by Local Proffit, Jr., and
"Guess What I Got In My Pocket?" by Little Fool. Several
pages were blank. Curious, Mustaine fed in a quarter and
punched up BB–174, "She-Bubba From Hell" by Victim. He
tapped his fingers impatiently on the plastic until the Zydeco
tune had ended. The jukebox whirred and clicked, the record
was jacked onto the turntable, and someone began to breath
glutinously in counterpoint to a raggedly strummed guitar.

After a few bars someone pulled the plug on the jukebox.
Its lights died; the turntable slowed, dragging the music into a
warped smear of sound. Some of the dancers were staring
with obvious enmity at Mustaine, who felt more out of his
element than before. Then the lights came back on, the
record was rejected, and a new one dropped into place.
Syrupy strings and a steel guitar. A few people started dancing
again and Miss Sedele pushed through the crowd at the edge

of the dance floor. She was pretty, crossing over into brittle, with slanty cheekbones, crow's-feet like faint scratches in soapstone forking from the corners of her pale green eyes, and a Lady Cruella mouth made fuller by an excess of lip gloss. Her hair was piled high with solitary stylish curls hanging down past her ears; her breasts were served up white and plump by the tight bodice of the green dress. She frowned at him, put her hands on her hips and said, "Well, I guess you had no way a'knowin'."

"No way a'knowing what?" said Mustaine with a measure of belligerence.

"Lotta these songs don't get played 'cept on special occasions."

"What occasions are we talking about?"

"Whenever I say it's an occasion." She took Mustaine's arm. "You lookin' frazzled, darlin'. Lemme getcha somethin' to smooth you out."

She led him to the bar, where Joe Dill and Tuyet were still playing poker dice. He flopped onto a stool next to Sedele, brushing against the kid with the guitar. Joe Dill leaned forward to peer at Mustaine and fixed him with a reproving stare. "I can't take you anywhere," he said.

Mustaine waved at the room, at all the din and blunder; the gesture made him feel drunker and gave him the sense of being more potent than his environment. "This is the best place in town? What's your idea of haute cuisine? Tastee Freeze?"

"You runnin' down my establishment?" Sedele asked with good humor; she signaled the bartender. "Give this boy a Cryptoverde, Earl."

"You gotta admit," said Mustaine, "the ambience is fucking weird. Sideshow Colonial Gothic."

Tuyet said, "Weird's normal in Grail. And normal—" she let her gaze swing toward Mustaine "—normal's not worth mentioning."

"You insecure about something?" he asked. "That why you such a bitch?"

"Now that's not called for," said Joe Dill.

Tuyet smiled triumphantly.

"Look," said Mustaine, trying to mend fences and at the same time uphold honor. "I'm grateful to you. But I'm not going to be anybody's leg-humper."

"Y'all ease back." Sedele spanked Joe Dill's hand. "The boy's had a tryin' day. And he's right. Just 'cause you befriended him don't give you no papers."

"Maybe he needs some company," Tuyet said with disdain. "Why don't you fix him up with Vida?"

Joe Dill said, "Yeah, that'd teach him 'bout weird."

Sedele turned on him. "Don't you go puttin' your mouth on Vida . . . not while I'm listenin'!"

There was a strained silence; the "Sultans of Swing" came from the jukebox; lean shadows were gracefully whirling in its glow, Cajun hearts were being broken.

"I won't have it," said Sedele grimly. "I won't have nobody talkin' down on Vida."

"Who's Vida?" Mustaine asked, intrigued by the name, by the effect it had produced.

Tuyet said something that sounded like "the Midsummer Queen," but Mustaine thought he must have misheard. Joe Dill, with what seemed equal parts reverence and spite, said, "You gotta know Vida to 'preciate her."

"Well," said Sedele, "that's somethin' you never gon' do, now is it, Joe? I mean you 'bout the last person she wants to get to know."

"I can think of a few others got less chance than me," he said.

They stared at one another, as emotionless and steadfast in their regard as the profiles on the Welcome to Grail sign. Finally Joe Dill swept up the poker dice and turned away. Tuyet whispered in his ear; he laughed and rolled the dice.

The bartender set down two green drinks crusted with foam. Sedele, anger still showing on her face, knocked back almost half of one. Mustaine had a sip. Tart and sweet, a little like a Margarita, but headier.

"What all's in this?" he asked, holding the glass up to his eyes. Threads of golden pulp were floating near the top;

against the glare from the ceiling, it seemed to contain a slow play of green light and shadow.

"Little a'this, little a'that," said Sedele shortly; then she appeared to relax. "Vodka, bamboo liqueur, gator bile, a dead gambler's cologne. Anything else green I could think of."

He smiled at that, but she remained deadpan.

" 'Course," she said, "there's a secret ingredient or two."

He studied the glass again.

"Go 'head and drink up," she said. "Two or three'll give you a whole new perspective . . . I swear."

He had another, longer swallow. "That what it does for you?"

"Yes, indeed! 'Fore I started drinkin' Cryptoverdes I wasn't the least little bit psychic."

"Right."

"You don't believe it?"

"I'm willing to be convinced."

She swiveled about to face him. "Gimme somethin' to hold . . . somethin' personal. There." She pointed to his earring. "Gimme that."

He unscrewed the stud and passed the earring over; it glinted in her palm—the stylized face of a silver cat. She closed her hand around it, her eyelids drooped. She sighed and her breasts swelled from the green bodice.

"This is a gift," she said. "From a woman . . . an older woman. A lover. She's unhappy. I'm gettin' you did wrong by her somehow." Her eyes blinked open. "You stole somethin' from her."

Mustaine tried to snatch back the earring, but Sedele held it out of reach.

"I guess," she went on, "you didn't really steal it. Just sorta stole it. I can't figure it out, but it's what I'm gettin'." She squeezed the earring in her fist, pressed the fist to her forehead. "She forgives you. She knows it wasn't in you to be the way she wanted. But she's hopin' someday you'll see what you gave up with her and come back. 'Course you ain't never comin' back. You ain't that kind."

Mustaine held up the empty glass to the bartender. He felt

weary. The long-haired kid was showing off with some simple
slide licks on his metal guitar. A National steel guitar. It had
to be at least seventy years old. A Son House guitar. Chances
were, it had been played by men with real talent, real reasons
for playing. The kid didn't deserve it.

"Probably best for the lady you don't come back," said
Sedele. "You'd just mess 'er up again."

"Get off it, okay?" said Mustaine.

"I ain't gon' judge you, that's what you worried about. I'm
the last person to sit in judgment."

The bartender brought a fresh drink. Mustaine had a
swallow.

"Want to hear more?" Sedele asked.

"Not about that."

"Awright." She tossed the earring from one hand to the
other. "How 'bout I tell you 'bout your character?"

"Whatever."

She ran the ball of her thumb across the tiny silver face.
"You think you got a line on things makes you immune from
people, but you wide open, boy. What you think is armor ain't
nothin' but an invitation to arrows. You just lookin' to get
hurt, and when nothin' comes 'long to hurtcha, you find a
way to hurt yourself. That's what you like to call bein' tough-
minded."

Listening to her analysis, he finished the second drink.
She was saying nothing new, only that he was limited
emotionally, and he had known that for some time. What
interested him most was why she wished to make him out an
innocent. It was tactical, he was certain, and he began to
believe that her intent was seductive in character. By illuminating his supposed naiveté, she was posing before him,
establishing a sexual validity, making herself out to be someone of vast experience and insight, someone that he would
run to for heat and consolation.

"There's strength in you," Sedele went on. "Sometimes it's
a resource, but other times it's like you don't know how to tap
into it—that makes you act weak."

He was getting very drunk, but he was calm and gathered

in the midst of drunkenness, and he thought there might be something to what Sedele had said about Cryptoverdes giving you a new perspective. He pretended to listen, distant from her, yet engaged by the swells of her breasts in their silky green shells, the exaggerated femininity of her gestures. Behind her, Joe Dill and Tuyet were talking to an old man in work clothes. The jukebox was playing more Dire Straits. Mustaine felt lyrically submerged in the moment, that he had managed the transition from stranger to accomplice in strangeness.

Sedele noticed him looking at her breasts. "I'm queer," she said at last. "So don't go gettin' no ideas."

Mustaine was unfazed. "You mean you like girls?"

"Doesn't everyone?"

"You like guys too," he said. "So why'd you decide we weren't happening?"

She started to object, but he broke in.

"I been on the losing end of that decision too many times not to recognize it. Way I figure, you got worried you weren't going to be the one in control. You wanted it to be all your idea."

"You're a smug bastard!"

He widened his eyes, affecting astonishment. "You mean I was right? Must be I'm psychic."

She gave a hitch of her shoulder. "Stick around. Could be I'll change my mind."

"I doubt it."

"Honey, you don't know how much I love a challenge."

Her eyes were intricate. The green irises salted with gold, always shifting, as if the colors were awash beneath thin layers of crystal. Jungle and sunlight. Little fevers in them, little shivers and twitches.

She handed him the earring. "Better put that back on, darlin'. You ain't whole without it."

He threaded in the earring, tightened the stud; it was warm from her hand.

"Joe tells me you a musician," she said.

"We starting over now?"

"Just takin' a little sidestep. What you play?"

"Guitar."

She reached around him, tapped the long-haired kid on his shoulder. "Let the man borrow your guitar, Cody."

The kid eyed Mustaine sullenly, then passed him the National steel guitar. "It's heavy," he said. "Don't drop it." He held out fingerpicks and a slide.

"Well?" Sedele said as Mustaine rested the guitar across his knee. "Play me somethin'." She made a slashing gesture across her throat to Earl and a second later the jukebox died.

The guitar must have weighed twenty-five, thirty pounds: like a small dead child in his arms. There was a painting of a woman in a green bathing suit water-skiing on the curved back of the instrument; she was plowing through turquoise water, sending up a frothy wake. He dropped Cody's picks on the bar, pulled a flat pick from his shirt pocket, and fitted the slide to his ring finger left hand, then touched the strings. It was tuned to an open G—that suited him fine.

He'd intended to play a couple of show-off passages and hand the guitar back, but after thirty seconds or so the music began to enclose him, to become a place he could hide within . . . which was always the case when it was good, no matter what his reasons for playing, whether trying to impress a girl or a club owner or some roach with major label connections, or just sitting in a room alone and trying to hide from himself. He played an uptempo blues—you couldn't play much except blues on a National steel. It took too much pressure to hammer down on the strings, to bend and pluck them. The notes that issued from the resonator inside the steel body came out dull, like nickels dropped in a blind man's cup. You had to work to brighten them, you had to labor at it, and from that labor, from cracking open your calluses on the strings so that your blood trickled along the neck, from squeezing your eyes shut with effort, came the feeling of passionate striving that was the blues, and even if you weren't any good, what you played was never less than blue.

The music Mustaine made was nervous and wired, traveling music, the music of interrupted flight, of anxiety, a break-down of the moment, of his take on being stranded in Grail, this chicory-flavored nowhere that seemed itself to be in a state of breakdown, of imminent collapse. It referenced as well the working-class decay evidenced by Le Bon Chance, the more ornate sexual decay of its redheaded owner, and the startling presence of a beautiful woman in a white dress who was staring at him with disturbing intensity from the fringe of the crowd. Whenever he managed to figure his way out of a passage he'd gotten lost in, he gave a soft, satisfied grunt, and then he was off on the right road again, chasing the feeling that had put his feet on the road in the first place, the sense that he was almost in touch with something that would light him up and fill him with hot purpose forever if he could only push a little harder, reach the next level of invention, believing in it even though he knew the feeling would remain a desperate inch beyond his grasp and last only for as long as the music.

5
June 23 — 12:00 A.M.

*L*IKE SHE ALWAYS DID BEFORE ENTERING LE BON
Chance, Vida read the security company decal stuck to
the window glass beside the front door. Read it over a few
times the way a good Catholic might say her Hail Marys
before entering an unholy place. This Establishment
Protected By Dill Security Services, it said, and then in script
letters beneath: *What ye sow, so shall ye reap* . . . The door-
knob felt warm to her hand, as if there were a great burning
inside. She hesitated, thinking she might be better off back at
the cabin. Behind her, a group of boys leaning against two
adjacent cars parked in the lot were hassling two black
women quick-stepping past on the sidewalk. When they had
spotted Vida, their eyes stuck to her but they didn't say a
thing. Just tracked her as she crossed the lot with her head
down, wearing her nicest summer dress, white with a scoop
neckline and decorated with lime crescents.

She pushed through the door. The familiar bad smell of
the club. Artificial brimstone compounded of cigarette smoke
and cleaning agents. But instead of a confusion of music and

human noise, all she heard was a single guitar playing. She picked out the musician straightaway. A thin, lanky man with shaggy black hair, sitting on a barstool, hunched over a silver guitar. Sitting next to him was Sedele. The music was agitated, dancing like static, but it had a sweet melody at its heart that drew her closer. The man's face was lean, sharp-featured, but there was a softness in it, an old-soul energy; his eyes were a dark, dark blue. He wore a silver earring, like a drop of guitar metal soldered to his lobe. She moved closer yet, aware that people were staring at her. She didn't care, she was accustomed to such. The earring resembled a cat's face and she recognized by that sign, by all the signs, that he was an expression of the Nine Forms made flesh. The one she thought of as The Cunning, The Poet, The One-Eyed Jack, though its true name was Zedaial. The Great Cloud must have brought him. It must have heard her wish, her said-out-loud prayer for someone to save her from Marsh, and sent her its Trump.

The man finished playing; the crowd clapped and shouted. He seemed uncomfortable when Sedele patted his arm, pretending to approve of the music. What she was really doing—trying to steal his power, like rubbing a cat's back to cause a discharge of electricity—it angered Vida. She hurried over to stand by his side and glared at Sedele, who glanced up in surprise and said, "Vida! What you doin' out so late?" The man's eyes ranged over Vida's body—he was only a Form made flesh and thus had the base nature of a man. He put on an innocent, inquisitive look that she assumed he'd used on women many times before; but then his eyes locked onto hers and she felt the cool flow of him, the stream of his spirit arcing across the distance between them.

"What's your name?" she asked him.

The question appeared to surprise him—she decided he must not be aware of his higher nature.

"Jack . . . Jack Mustaine." He smiled, an expression that turned down one corner of his mouth the slightest bit and lifted the other corner high, as if he were trying not to smile but couldn't help it. She said the name to herself: Jack.

Another sign.

"Can I talk to you a while?" She eased past a long-haired kid and took the stool next to the man.

"Sure." He rested his right arm on the body of the silver guitar. "What you want to talk about?"

"I'm Vida Dumars," she said. "I own a little diner back down the road. I live out along Shotgun Row." A silence hedged the space between them, and she asked, "Where you live?"

"I haven't lived anywhere for a long time." He stroked the strings of the guitar—as if it were a gentled pet responding to the touch, it made a sweet sound.

"Where'd you come from, then?"

"West coast. LA."

From the west—like the Great Cloud. Vida noticed that Sedele had moved down along the bar and was talking to Joe Dill and his Vietnamese witch. The long-haired kid and the two girls he'd been talking to had also moved farther away. All of them worried her luck would spill over onto them.

"That where you were born . . . LA?" she asked.

"No, I was born elsewhere."

"Ain'tcha gonna tell me?"

"Back east," he said. "I'm a Leo, Scorpio rising. What's your sign?"

"I don't believe in that foolishness."

"Me neither. But I thought I should get to ask one question."

"You don't have to talk smooth to get what you want," she told him. "All you hafta do is speak the truth."

He looked nonplussed. "Which truth is that? The absolute, the momentary? The gospel unadorned?"

"The momentary."

"You're confusing me," he said. "And that's all three kinds."

She might have liked the answer if he were only a man, but as things stood she felt less sure about him.

"But I'm just passing through," he added. "I won't be confused much longer."

That he knew he was only passing through the flesh made her feel easier about him. "Where you stayin' at?" she asked. "The Gulfview?"

"I haven't got a room yet. But if it's close by, that's probably where I'll stay."

The jukebox kicked up a racket, and Bruce Springsteen started singing about how he had a hungry heart. Couples went back to dancing, but were keeping an eye on Vida all the while.

The man sang along softly with the chorus then said to Vida, "You like that song?" She realized the Form would surely know her heart and how it hungered for liberation of every sort—that hunger had brought her to trouble in the past, but she believed if she were ever going to get clear of trouble, it would be the engine that carried her away.

"I don't much care for music," she said. "But the words are all right."

Puzzlement cut a vertical line in his brow, running a half-inch up from the bridge of his nose. "I thought you liked my playing . . . that's why you came over."

"That wasn't it."

He picked out a scatter of notes on the guitar that had the feel of a sardonic sentence. "I heard about you from Sedele and them." He jerked his head toward where Sedele and Joe Dill were sitting.

"It's all true," she said. "Whatever they told you."

"They just said you're weird. But you don't seem weird to me. Unusual, maybe."

"How'm I unusual?"

He dropped his pitch half an octave and said in a slowed-down sexy voice, "I haven't put my finger on it yet."

"You ain't never gonna *put your finger on it*, you don't start treatin' me real."

"Hey, give me a break," he said. "I'm just trying to impress you with my *savoir faire*."

"You already impressed me. But every time you open your mouth I'm gettin' less impressed. I told you, you don't have to sell me nothin'."

"If I can't use my good material, I'm not going to have a whole lot to say. 'Least not 'til I get to know you."

"That's good. I hear you a lot better when you not sayin' nothin'."

The bartender asked Vida if she wanted something, and she said, "No." She'd never had dealings with any of the Nine Forms before now, and maybe, she thought, they always interacted with you as man to woman, woman to man. She supposed that was how you had to treat them in turn.

Jack cocked his head to the side, as if to see her more clearly, then considered the strings of the guitar. He fingered one, but didn't pluck it. His ocean-colored eyes engaged her again and held. She saw down to the place inside him that the Form wanted her to swim to. Love had to come, she realized, or else the Form couldn't emerge to help her.

The notion of love nettled Vida. It wasn't that difficult a spell to work. Jack was a good-looking man and the fact that the Form had chosen him to be its horse while in the flesh, to convey it through the world, meant he was a worthy vessel. She had seen enough of him and understood enough about her own predilections to know that she could work that change in both of them. She had his eye already and his soul was ready to follow. But love was ever a struggle. It took a mustang heart to survive the race it ran. Vida wasn't sure she was up to the task—but what choice was there? She could remain in Grail, plagued by Marsh and his dream weaponry, or she could let the Form enfold her and carry her away.

"You can stay with me," she said.

He said, "What?"

She slid off the barstool. "Y'gotta car?"

His perplexity deepened. "It broke down out on the highway. I guess it's getting repaired."

"We can take my pickup then. It's back at the diner."

It seemed he wanted to express doubt concerning this arrangement, but his higher nature prevailed and he came to his feet. He offered the silver guitar to the long-haired kid, but Joe Dill sang out above the music, "Hey, Cody!"

The kid, about to take the guitar, stopped with his hand out and said, "Yeah?"

"Let the man hang onto it a day or two." Joe Dill ambled over, the Vietnamese woman at his shoulder. "He plays it a helluva lot better'n you. Maybe he'll play us some more 'fore he leaves."

"It's worth over a thousand dollars," Cody said querulously.

"I'm good for it," Joe Dill said. "Ol' Jack ain't goin' nowhere 'til they fix his Beamer."

"Hey," Jack said. "It's okay. I got my own guitar."

Joe Dill bullied Cody with his eyes. Finally Cody said, "Naw, man. Go ahead. It's cool."

Jack glanced back and forth between them, shrugged, and said, "Whatever."

The Springsteen song ended.

Vida caught Sedele staring hotly at her and turned away, not because she was unnerved, but because she didn't want to deal with that sad, intense look. Out of the corner of her eye she saw Sedele heave a sigh and walk off toward the jukebox.

Everyone was watching them now. Old men, a boy at the pool table, the dancers. Jack's face tightened. The Form had let him bear witness to the evil here, Vida thought.

Joe Dill made a benediction with his right hand, sketched the sign of the cross in midair, smiling a humorless smile that turned the gesture into a mockery.

"Be fruitful and multiply," he said.

On her stool, the Vietnamese witch rolled the poker dice across the polished surface of the bar and laughed at the result.

As they reached the entrance Jack opened the door and put a hand lightly on Vida's lower back to guide her through. The touch gave her a thrill, a little electric surge that rippled down into her buttocks and between her legs.

Love starting its run.

A synth beat issued from the jukebox; a man's voice muttering, the words not quite audible, but menacing

nonetheless, and then a woman began to scream, crying out
to God at first, but the screams losing their shape, becoming
agonized howls and whimpers, and the man continuing to
mutter, as if he were cursing a screaming engine that he was
tinkering with, dissatisfied with its performance.

Vida cast a look back as the door swung shut behind them.
Saw Sedele leaning against the jukebox, arms folded. A
wicked emerald flicker surfaced in her left eye. Then the door
closed with a *snick* and they were alone.

6

June 23—After Midnight

As THE PICKUP RATTLE-BANGED AND JOUNCED OVER the rutted road leading to the Gulf, Mustaine sat half-turned to Vida behind the wheel. Her face aglow in the dashboard lights, the sheen of sweat on the upper slopes of her breasts glowing as well. He'd been hit on by women before, but never in quite this way. Her utter lack of camouflage, the absence of attitude—it was as if she'd perceived a quality in him that not even he could see and decided that it qualified him in some way. She was sure enough beautiful, but it wasn't beauty that had moved him off his barstool. There was a heaviness about Vida, an apparent weight to her soul that caused him to trust her perceptions, to half-believe there might be something inside him worth noticing. It seemed everyone in Le Bon Chance held the same view. Why else all the attention given her by the crowd? Why else would Joe Dill and Tuyet and Sedele have spoken about her as they had? Their regard, full of envy and longing and wariness, had been an acknowledgment of sorts, marking her as someone of unusual worth, and this tended to validate for Mustaine both

her intuitions and her feelings—still unspoken yet sensed—
about him.

Her eyes flicked toward him; a tenth of a smile rearranged
the curve of her lips. "What you gawkin' at?"

"I don't get you," he said.

"I thought I was pretty straightforward. What don't you
get?"

"The straightforward part, I guess. I'm not used to it."

The pickup dipped into a pothole, and Mustaine bounced
so high, his head bumped the roof. Out the window he saw
marshy ground covered with tall grasses, a poison green
under a moon just past full, and a broken fenceline of cypress
to the east. The smell of brine pierced an overarching odor of
sweet rot.

"You hungry?" Vida asked. "I can fix you up somethin'."

Mustaine said no thanks.

"Don't look so worried," she said. "It's just a night. Whatever comes, I got to open the diner tomorrow mornin', and
you got to take care of your business." The wind combed
strands of hair across her mouth; she pursed her lips and blew
them away. "World'll keep on spinnin'."

Everything she said had such a forthright character, it shut
down all his glibness. He started to ask what she was doing
here, a woman like her in a shithole like Grail; he'd expect to
find her in penthouse Manhattan, a Malibu beach house. He
recognized that with a few words and an invitation, she had
reduced him to clichés.

"What was all that back at the bar?" he asked after a pause.
"People staring at you like . . . like I don't know. I couldn't tell
what was going on."

She took her time in answering, wrangling the wheel to
the right and sending the pickup swerving around a bend. "I
got a history with this town. It's complicated."

He mulled this over.

She darted her eyes toward him. "It ain't all what you're
thinking."

"What was I thinking?"

"That maybe I was promiscuous. That's how I used to be. But I haven't been with anyone for more'n three years now."

"Jesus! You don't hold back, do you?"

"That's my place there." Vida pointed to a cabin of weathered unpainted boards with a tar-papered roof no more than a stone's throw from the curving shore of the Gulf, set on a patch of cleared ground. Mowed lawn and a live oak off to one side, its crown nearly leafless, moss bearding the bare lower branches. An avenue of moonlight dwindled toward the horizon, dividing the dark placid waters. To the east, a hundred yards from the cabin, a stand of trees and brush that blended in with the picket line of cypress.

Vida pulled up on the shoulder beside the cabin; the engine dieseled for a while after she cut the ignition. She hopped out, saying, "C'mon," and strode toward the porch steps, the skirt of her white dress swaying like a rung bell. Mustaine grabbed the National steel by the neck and followed. A light went on inside as he climbed the steps, illuminating a long living room sparsely furnished with two rocking chairs, a dove-gray sofa fronted by a wood-and-glass coffee table, and a china closet containing an assortment of voodoo dolls. In one corner a console TV, its screen over-painted by the image of a black medieval sun with a scowling face and stylized spiky rays. Hooked throw rugs lay on the dirt-colored floorboards like puddles of bright red, green, and yellow water banded in concentric rings. Mardi Gras prints on the wall: impressionistic scenes of bacchanal. Stack of paperbacks on the table, all dealing with the interpretation of dreams.

Mustaine heard Vida rattling pans in the kitchen. He parked the guitar on the sofa and went to see. She was standing at the sink, transferring cutlery and dishes and pans into a counter rack. Her chestnut hair spilled across her shoulders. A pretty country wife at her chores. Strange-looking designs of red and green lines on the sides of the woodstove.

"Rest yourself," she said. "I'll only be a minute."

There were no interior doors in the cabin. Standing in the front room, Mustaine could see straight through to the

kitchen and then to the bedroom at the rear, to a wide brass
bed beneath a high window, its blue coverlet decorated with
crescent moons and white roses. From the outside the cabin
had looked rundown, but the furniture was good quality,
expensive, and the minimalism of the decorating scheme
made the age-darkened boards appear part of the design.
She'd put some work into the place. He thought that if he had
entered the cabin not knowing who lived there, he would
have imagined the occupant to be a yuppie who ran a business in New Orleans and only came to Grail on the odd
weekend. None of it matched up with his impression of Vida,
which, though still diffuse, suggested that she might have a
more casual and old-fashioned approach to interior decora-
tion. All the voodoo stuff, the books on dreams—likely they
weren't window dressing, but articles of faith, and that jibed
with his take on her. But he had expected a sloppier, cozier
environment, not rooms that might be featured in an article
about renovated slave cabins in the Sunday supplement of
the *Picayune*.

He wandered back outside and sat on the bottom step.
Watching moonlight shimmer on the water and grasses
rippling in the breeze nudged him toward peace. The moon,
still low above the Gulf, resembled a glob of melted silver, its
surface chased with a scattering of gray punch marks. Halfway
to the horizon, a tiny constellation of red and purple riding
lights established the passage of a shrimp boat. The tide
sloshed lazily against the bank and something large, maybe a
night-fishing bird, splashed in the offing. Fireflies danced in
the dark blue air. Vida came down the steps and sat beside
him, smoothing out the white skirt beneath her. He caught
her fresh scent; the pressure of her hip warmed him.

"Want your guitar?" she asked. "I can bring it."

"Thought you didn't like my playing."

She shook back a fall of hair from her face. "I don't like
much happens in Le Bon Chance. That's why I dragged you
outa there."

"Then how come you went there?"

"I was lonesome. Lonesome takes what it can get."

He was having trouble thinking of something to say, and that was new for him; he understood how to talk to women, how to make them laugh and turn off their caution. But cleverness seemed out of place now. He felt a tension, a tentativeness, that he hadn't felt before.

"Tell me about your history," he said at last. "With the town."

"It's just a buncha ugly. They used to call me a whore. Now they call me crazy. Guess they expected more out of me 'cause I was Midsummer Queen."

"Yeah, Tuyet said something . . . What's up with that?"

"It's a big tradition 'round here. Every twenty years they choose a ten-year-old girl to be Midsummer Queen. She's the luck of the town. She draws all the bad luck to herself so Grail can prosper." She gave a wry laugh. "Must have took with me, 'cause I haven't had much good luck. But they expect their Queens to be upstandin'. Solid citizens. They worry they mighta picked the wrong girl for the job. 'Cause if the Good Gray Man don't find her suitable, the bad luck'll return."

"They don't believe in that shit?"

"Sure they do. People 'round here been believing it for a couple hundred years. The founders of Grail made a deal with somebody they called the Good Gray Man. Some kinda spirit that's supposed to be hangin' around these parts. He promised good fortune to the town 'long as they kept up the tradition of the Midsummer Queen. Anyway, you can learn about it for yourself come tomorrow evenin'. They'll be choosin' my successor."

"You don't believe it, though?"

"I don't care 'bout it one way or another. I got a lot worse'n bad luck doggin' me."

She rested an elbow on one knee, cupped her chin, gazing out at the Gulf water, flat and glossy as a polished tabletop. A firefly settled in her hair, shining through a stray curl. Her profile limned by light spilling through the doorway. Looking at her, Mustaine experienced a heart twinge, a little break in rhythm. The way he felt, alerted to her yet thickheaded, as if drugged—it made no sense.

"Funny how you know things," she said. "It's like somethin' sleepin' inside you wakes up and spies somethin' exactly like itself wakin' in somebody else. It don't have to be 'bout nothin'. It's just funny is all." The whites of her eyes shined in the half-dark. "You might wanna say somethin' 'bout now, else I'm gonna feel stupid."

"I don't know what to make of it," he said.

"You never been attracted to a woman of a sudden before?"

"Not like this."

She took his hand, rubbed her thumb across his knuckles. Cicadas sawed out in the high grasses, a papery-sounding chorus like children with kazoos. The breeze strengthened, raised up a rushing noise. It seemed that Mustaine heard shreds of a brighter music on the wind, skeins of wild guitar and billows of accordion.

"Let's go on inside," said Vida. "Talkin' won't make nothin' much happen."

7

Before Dawn

*M*AKING LOVE GENERALLY SERVED TO ARMOR VIDA against the arrows of her insecurity. She had been schooled in the art, and she was comfortable with the pleasurable uses of her body. Under ordinary circumstances, with ordinary partners, men whom she turned to for solace, lovemaking became a passionate exercise whose aim was to blunt the sharpness of the world. But that night she was connected to Jack, to the Form that lived through him, and brought true passion to the act. The arch in her back as she straddled him was put there by a yielding, a surrender of self to a sweeter service than her own pleasure. She clenched the brass head-rail with both hands, squeezing until it squeaked. Her hips hammered down and her flesh felt like hot oil under pressure, flowing from shape to shape. She moaned in harmony with the wind that blew hard off the Gulf, using the cabin for a wooden trumpet to sound its sobbing vowels, and afterward, lying with her head on Jack's shoulder, she had the notion she was protected, that love had come enough into their hearts to guarantee her freedom from Marsh. All the signs were auspi-

cious. Wind shook the cabin and the picture of Sacred Heart
Jesus on her bedroom wall tilted to the right and remained
cockeyed, suspended by the blessing of He who it depicted.
The rattling glassware atop the refrigerator chimed a gentle,
intermittent music; the Guidry's yellow dog bayed three times
as if to announce a change it felt but could not comprehend.
From where she lay, the four panes of the window above her
bed resembled a block of postage stamps, each appearing to
contain a rectangle of blue darkness with a single white star
burning in its upper left-hand corner, testifying to the con-
gruity of human will and heavenly purpose.

Jack propped himself on an elbow, looked down at her.
"Want to tell me what you're thinking?"

"Nothin' you haven't heard before. Just I feel good . . .
safe." His face was in shadow; she reached up and ruffled his
hair. "How 'bout you?"

"I got about fifty, sixty dozen things going on."

"Say some of 'em."

"Well . . . I was trying to figure out who you are."

"That'll take a while . . . for both of us. But we made a
beginning, and that's the trickiest part. What else?"

He left a pause, then said, "I'm falling in love with you. I
don't understand it."

Vida felt that same fall inside herself, but knew it would be
best not to say the words—he would fall deeper and deeper
until she said them, and when she did, when she couldn't
stand not to say them anymore, that would stop his fall and
that was the depth of love they would be stuck at. She
intended to wait a long time with Jack.

"Why not?" she asked. "It's what happens sometimes."

"Not to me . . . not 'til now."

"Well, don't worry it to death, all right?"

She linked her arms around his neck and hauled him
down so he lay half atop her and kissed his mouth, softly at
first, then losing herself.

"That stuff you were doing," he said, breaking from the
kiss. "When you were on top?"

"Stuff?"

"You know. The way you were squeezing me."

"Oh, that," she said. "I learned all that when I was four-teen. My cousin Amelia bought this woman's magazine had an article . . . 'How to Exercise Your Love Muscle.' We practiced every day 'til we got pretty good at it. Difference was, Amelia was savin' it for the man she was goin' to marry. Me, I couldn't wait to try it out. I earned myself quite a reputation."

"I bet."

"Didn't you ever have a woman do that for you?"

"Yeah, but not quite so . . ."

"Not quite so what?"

He looked embarrassed. "So expertly."

"Told you I had a history. It don't bother you, does it?"

"No . . . hell. But you keep taking me by surprise."

"I got a few more surprises. Just you wait'll tomorrow."

"Why wait 'til then?"

"I gotta go to work in a couple hours! I'm gon' be draggin' as it is. But you can sleep in. I'll catch a ride into town and leave you the pickup. When you wake, come on over the diner. I'll fix you breakfast."

He settled himself beside her so they lay face-to-face and placed a hand on her cheek. The touch brought a wave of sleepiness—the Form granting her its peace.

"Vida," he said.

"Mmmm. What?"

"Nothing."

He gathered her into his arms and she nestled against him, feeling the tug of dreams, no longer wary of them. She slept hard at first, gone deeper than dreams into her own darkness, and when she surfaced the dream that came was bright and calm. She was walking naked in an orchard of trees with golden leaves and glass fruit. The grass, too, was golden, and a tiger with gemmy eyes padded along beside her. The leaves of the lower branches trailed across her skin, leaving glowing lip-shaped marks whose warmth faded like the warmth of kisses. Winged emeralds disguised as June bugs flashed back and forth. Then in a clearing ahead she saw an armored knight all of glass standing above a slain beast. The belly of the beast, mounded high as a hillock, was gashed and bleeding, and the gauntlets of the knight were gloved in blood, as if he had reached inside the wounds to bring forth some fleshy treasure. The sight was at odds with the serenity of the orchard. Vida had no sense that the knight was Marsh, yet she knew it must be him, and that she was the beast he was pillaging. She took a step back, afraid he would spot her. But the tiger leaped forward, shattering the knight into a thousand shards with a single blow, then proceeded to lick the blood from the broken glass until no sign of her enemy remained, apart from a glittering wreckage among the grass blades that appeared no more threatening than a bright scattering of pollen or a crystalline residue of time.

8

Breakfast

*V*IDA'S MOONLIGHT DINER HAD FIVE EARLY BREAKFAST regulars: four old men who sat at the end of the counter slurping oatmeal and peering down Vida's neckline when she served them, and fat, bald, red-faced John Guineau, the editor of the *Grail Seeker*, who came each morning at a quarter to eight and sat in the booth nearest the door—though he scarcely fit into it, a slab of his pin-striped stomach overlapping onto the tabletop—and read his own newspaper while risking cardiac arrest by eating four sausage patties and a large plate of French fries, and downing three cups of chicory-flavored coffee. They had all known her since she was a bulge in her mama's belly, but they rarely engaged her in conversation. Which was fine with Vida. She liked quiet mornings. Liked the sun slanting through the Venetian blinds onto the Formica counter, the smell of bacon frying, and the shine on the grill. She would have never thought she'd enjoy running a diner, but she had learned to relish the routine and the continuity of faces, the same day after day except for the occasional tourist and long-hauler. It had come to be her natural element, the place where she felt most protected from Marsh, too involved with the clutter of business to pay attention to his manipulations of her thoughts. But as she prepared to bring Guineau his breakfast that morning, on turning to pick up his fries, instead of potatoes she saw a writhing heap of tiny men and women, naked, their skins golden-brown, entangled in a complexity of sexual congress on the white plate. She put a hand to her mouth to stop an outcry, but was unable to take her eyes off the miniature orgy . . . an orgy that was, she thought, likely happening right now at Marsh's penthouse, and he was inviting her to reclaim her rightful place at the squirming center of his show. She heard Guineau calling to her, saying he could use his food, and she lifted the plate, careful not to touch its contents, and carried it over to the booth.

"You slow this mornin', girl." Guineau plucked up a tiny nubile woman with golden tresses, her legs kicking, and popped her into his pink mouth.

Chewed.

Vida stared in horror as he doused the humping bodies with ketchup, then picked up a lovemaking couple and bit them in half while still joined. She backed away, fetched up against the counter.

"Hell's wrong with you, Vida?" Guineau grabbed his fork and impaled two slim golden-brown men out of a daisy chain and sucked them off the tines.

"Just the heat's got me flustered."

"It ain't hot." Guineau dunked a young girl headfirst into the ketchup bottle, twirled her around long enough to drown her, and chomped off her limp dripping-red torso. "Might be hot for tourists, but not if you Louisiana-bred. Maybe you got a touch of fever, you."

Vida retreated into the kitchen, leaned against the freezer until her heart stopped racing. Anson, the cook, grinned at her from the stove, his round black face glowing with sweat; he gestured at the freezer.

"Woman, you gon' hafta crawl inside that thing, you wanna stay cool," he said.

She waved dismissively. "I needed a break from watchin' John Guineau eat."

"I hear that. One of these days they gon' hafta use the Jaws of Life to pry his ass outa that booth."

She gathered herself, took a deep breath, and went back out into the front, avoiding even a glance at Guineau. She gave the four old men a refill of their coffee; they watched her pour with enfeebled gratitude and enervated lust. The oldest, Toby Abijean, had spilled his oatmeal, and moved to kindness she mopped it up, bending low to provide them a thrill. They stared with rheumy eyes, slurped and wheezed, and once she had finished they returned to their gaspy conversation.

Guineau had cleaned his plate of fries. He unwedged himself from the booth, swatted at his belly with the napkin, and heaved over to the register; he plunked down exact change plus a two-dollar tip on the cash tray and said, "Fries were extra good this mornin', Vida. You do somethin' special with 'em?"

"Naw," she said shakily.

"Well, they were extra good. Whatever you didn't do, don't do it again."

He chuckled at his joke and gave her a pat on the arm. A few seconds later the bell above the door jingled at his exit. Vida left his table uncleared. She checked to make sure the old men were all set, then stepped into the larder and opened a gallon tin of peaches. As she pried at the lid, her eyes went to the shelves — it was as if she had been transported life-sized inside a dollhouse skyscraper and was looking at a cross-section of three floors . . . the floors of Clifford Marsh's penthouse, populated by his sycophants. A menagerie of male and female creatures dressed for a masked ball. Gathered in small groups. Gesturing. Alive. Glittering two-legged birds with bared breasts; men in comic opera military uniforms; a hunchback with a priapic mask who scuttled about butting people in the rear end with his obscene nose; a girl of no more than twelve, naked except for the fact that her flesh was covered with painted words such as Cunt, Sodomize, Fuck. Vida had seen it all before; it was typical of Marsh's parties.

She gazed dully at the scene, accepting that he had penetrated her last refuge, that he could now find her anywhere.
Then she spotted him. Standing at the edge of the third floor.
A miniature silver-haired devil in a tuxedo, with a grinning
tanned face almost unmarked by time. Looking at her. He
waved gaily, then beckoned. Seized by hatred, she reached
out for him, but before she could close her fist, he and all the
rest had misted away, replaced by boxes of soda crackers and
cans of tomato sauce.

Despairing, Vida rested her brow against a shelf. She
thought about Jack and the thought strengthened her. If she
could get away from Grail. If she could just get away. She
swallowed, closed her eyes, straightened. It felt as if something was flapping inside her head, troubling her concentration. "God," she said, the word sighing out. She took hold of
the can of peaches and pried up the lid. The can was empty
of peaches. She might have been looking through a ceiling
peephole into Marsh's bedroom. At the bottom of the can was
a bed with a black satin coverlet on which her younger self
reclined naked, a white shape that from her apparent height
resembled an old-fashioned keyhole in a black door with a
strong light shining through it. A dozen men, also naked,
ringed the bed. They were vigorously stroking themselves,
preparing to soil her.

She shrieked and knocked the can onto the floor. Peaches
everywhere. Puddled syrup. She slipped in the syrup and
nearly fell. She screamed in rage, in terror, and began ripping
down boxes and cans from the shelves. Crackers and salt and
mustard mired with the syrup. She collapsed in a corner, staring at the mess she'd made. A knock sounded on the larder
door. Anson called out, "Vida?" When she didn't respond, he
tried again.

"I'm okay," she said.

"Some man here to see you," Anson said.

Marsh, she thought. He had sent his demon.

"He say you promise to fix him breakfas'."

Jack.

"Tell him . . ." She pulled herself to her feet. "Tell him I'll be a minute."

She fixed her face, using a labelless can for a mirror, and on her way through the kitchen, she told Anson to hustle up a Cajun omelet and bacon. Jack was sitting in the last booth, facing away from the old men. She brought him coffee, kissed his cheek, and sat opposite him.

"You all right?" he asked. "You look a little ragged."

"Now you to blame for that, ain'tcha?" She put on a smile she did not feel. She wanted to tell him about Marsh, but believed that might scare him off before the Form could fully manifest. "What you plannin' on doin' today?"

"Beats me. Maybe sit on a bench and spit tobacco. I'll fit right in." His blue eyes seemed to find the fear inside her and give it a caress. "You still like me this morning?"

She restrained herself from saying she loved him—it wasn't time yet. "I like you fine," she said. "Maybe even a little more'n that."

"I was thinking the same about you." He rested his arms on the back of the booth, as if draping them over the shoulders of two invisible friends. "So you going to fix me breakfast?"

"Believe me, you'll eat a lot better you let Anson do the fixin'." She glanced toward the kitchen. The old men were peering at them, probably trying to imprint Jack on their memories, polishing the story they would tell about Vida and her new man.

The kitchen door swung open—Anson came out carrying two plates. He ambled over, gazed suspiciously at Jack, and set the plates in front of him. Jack said, "Hey, thanks," and Anson said to Vida, "You need somethin' else, jus' give a holler, you."

As Jack ate, Vida studied the way his jaw muscles clumped, the cording of his neck. "Where were you headin'?" she asked. " 'Fore your car broke down?"

"Florida." He dabbed at his mouth with a napkin. "New Smyrna Beach. Friend of mine's letting me use his beach house for a few months. I've been wanting to do some writing, and that'll be a good place for it."

"Writin' music, you mean?"

"Songs." He forked up a bite of omelet and chewed. "This is great!"

"Anson's a treasure," Vida said absently. "That what you do for a livin'? Write songs?"

"Mmm-hmm." He swallowed the bite. "I can sell songs all right, but nobody wants to hear me sing 'em. My voice isn't that strong."

"I think you got a nice voice."

"Only time you ever heard me sing is last night. Anybody can sound decent singing along with a record."

"Well, let me hear somethin'."

"Now?"

"Nobody's gon' be listenin' 'cept me. Those old men wouldn't hear a bomb goin' off."

Jack set down his fork. "I didn't bring a guitar."

"Don't have to be much. Just give me a taste."

"Okay," he said. "But it'd be better with a guitar."

He closed his eyes and sang. The song was a ballad, and his voice was whispery, so sweet and soft it took Vida by surprise and she didn't connect with the words until he was halfway through a verse:

> ". . . maybe I'm a dreamer, maybe I'm a fo-ool,
> Maybe I'm just a lonely ma-an
> But maybe I got the answers to
> Those questions that are troublin' you . . .
> All you gotta do is ask . . ."

He tapped out a reggae rhythm on the edge of the table as he hit the chorus:

> "You can't hide your love from me,
> You can't hide your love from me . . .
> Well, you can run but . . .
> You can't hide your love from me . . ."

Jack broke the song off abruptly, looking uncomfortable. "It needs a guitar," he said.

"Oh, dear!" Vida pretended to fan herself. "I'd be embarrassed to tell you what sort of physical reaction I just had."

"Yeah, right!" he said, but she could see he was pleased.

"Bet the girl you wrote it for like to fell over backwards when you sang it to her."

"I wrote that this morning," he said. "Not long after you left."

She felt herself blushing, pleasurably confused. "For me? You wrote it for me?"

He nodded.

She scrambled to call up the words, the message the Form was sending her. . . . *maybe I got the answers to / all the questions that are troubling you / all you gotta do is ask* . . . It needed guidance, it needed her to come a step forward.

He caressed her elbow. "Say something."

"I'm overwhelmed."

"Nobody wrote you a song before?"

She shook her head. "Guess I never gave nobody a chance to feel like writin' one."

A green low-slung sports car wound out past the diner, raising dust from the shoulder, gaining speed as it headed for the city limits sign and the speed trap beyond.

"Well," Jack said. "I might have a few more for you."

It seemed to Vida that her focus kept having to shift a shorter distance between Jack and the Form. They were becoming the same. Knowing that lent her some courage. She had only to get through another day or so. Then the Form would be manifest, and it would carry her away.

"You still headin' for New Smyrna Beach . . . when you leave?"

"Depends," he said, meeting her eyes. "We might have to talk about that."

"God, I hope you got some idea what you gettin' into."

He grinned. "Not a clue."

"I got serious trouble. People say I'm crazy. I wish that was all of it, but it's not. I pissed off the wrong people."

"What are you talking about?"

"You'll think I'm crazy."

"No, I won't."

"You will!" She snapped the words, then her tone softened. "You will . . . I know it. There's times I think it sounds crazy, me."

The door jingled. Two long-haired men in T-shirts and jeans, trucker wallets chained to their belts, took stools at the counter; the old men gazed at them anxiously.

"I gotta work." Vida fingered a pen and order book from her apron pocket.

He put a hand on her wrist, lightly restraining her. "I want to know everything about you. Nothing you say is going to change how I feel."

She saw the Form peering out at her from the shadows in his eyes. "All right. But I hope you mean it, 'cause this is gonna give it a test."

9

Magic Time

OCCUPYING HALF A GLASS STOREFRONT ON EAST Monroe was a shop with the word REMEDIES rendered in gilt stick-on letters at the center of a clear oval; the remainder of the window had been spray-painted black, embellished with silver ankhs, golden crescents and stars, and various arcana that Mustaine could not identify. Smaller letters on the door inscribed the legend:

NEDRA HAWES
Oracles and Psychic Divination

The other half of the building was given over to something called Say Cheese! The blinds being drawn, Mustaine could not determine whether the name signified a photographer's studio or a cheese shop. Either way, he thought, this confluence of the mystical and the mundane reaffirmed his opinion that in Grail these two apparently opposing systems were both conjoined and clearly demarked, like puzzle pieces that fitted together yet depicted separate elements of an overall design.

He peered in through the clear oval of the remedy shop window and in the gloomy interior made out display cases, mounted shelves, an ajar door from which a fan of yellow lamplight spread. He tried the door and found it unlocked, but decided against entering. What would he do once inside? Perform some act of mockery? Buy a geechee charm? He leaned against the parking meter out front, facing toward Le Bon Chance, which was situated down a ways and across the street. The grubbiness of white cement block and dead neon dice and empty gravel lot exposed by the strong sun. Now and again a car zipped past, heading for Biloxi and points east. An elderly black man in a pink long-sleeved dress shirt and worn overalls, with a ladies floppy-brimmed straw hat shading his face, came limping along the sidewalk, followed by a hinge-gaited hound with a blue bandanna knotted about its neck. Mustaine recalled a bass player who had auditioned for his band in LA; he, too, had dressed his dog in a bandanna. When he failed to make the band, he had assaulted the drummer's girlfriend, accusing her of casting a spell and thus causing him to play poorly. Mustaine had since held a jaundiced view of dogs with bandannas.

As the black man passed, Mustaine said, "What's up?" and the man, without looking up, said, "Muthafucka gon' kill our ass, he get heah befo' Wednesday."

"Right," said Mustaine, turning his gaze back along the road.

Lethargy, he thought, would be considered uptempo in Grail.

Overhead, the sky was cloudless, but to the west lay a pile of bubbling white cumulus. Weird-looking. Like the wreckage of a wedding cake, with a frothy ledge of leaden gray circling the base that appeared to be changing shape more quickly than the mass above it, as if the two areas of cloud were being affected by different streams of wind. He watched it drift townward, thinking about the story Vida had told him.

The crazy story.

A woman like Vida, stuck in a creep show like Grail—she

was bound to get squirrely. But she was basically sound. Strong. Her soul came busting out at you like an ocean wave. All she needed, he thought, was someone to take responsibility while she backed down the stress levels. He wasn't secure, however, with the idea that he might be the right someone. Responsibility had never been his strength, though his stability wasn't in question. Despite a multiplicity of career and personal traumas, he had remained annoyingly stable. A nervous breakdown would do wonders for his self-esteem, reinvigorate a sense of his humanity. He had been skating along for years. Uninvolved with family, unaffected by friends, as if damaged by an accident he could not recall. Spiritually neutered. But he felt a pull from Vida, an undertow of emotion dragging him toward her, and he wanted to go with it. His first agent in LA, a psychotherapy junkie, had treated him to a month of sessions with a shrink, who asked him after the fourth appointment if he would be scheduling a fifth. When Mustaine said he would not, the shrink offered a preliminary diagnosis, opining that he seemed emotionally disconnected and could use some more work.

"Of course you might get lucky," the shrink said.

Mustaine said, "Lucky?"

"The world has a way of reconnecting people. Sometimes the reconnection is . . . difficult. Traumatic in the extreme. Sometimes, though—" the shrink swiveled his chair around and looked down onto Rodeo "—it's not so bad."

"You see lots of that, do you?" Mustaine asked. "Reconnection."

"No," said the shrink, with a quick shake of his head. "Not around here."

Mustaine imagined this thing with Vida might be the beginning of a "traumatic in the extreme" reconnection, or maybe even a "not so bad" one. His initial instincts had been to back off, to analyze, but she had rolled over him and he doubted free will was a viable option at this point.

The heat began cooking an asphalt smell from the blacktop; the remnants of something wrapped in crumpled newspaper and tossed into the gutter was attracting flies. Mustaine considered going back to the cabin and sleeping a while longer. He thought about retracing his path up Monroe and taking a stroll through Crosson's Hardware, the only other store open at this hour. Check out the skill saws. The belt sanders.

Remedies, he decided.

The interior of the shop was cool and dim, smelling of herbal bitterness. Stocking the cases and lining the shelves were apothecary bottles with hand-written labels, filled with dark fluids. Also charms made of bones, feathers, beads, and scraps of fur. Medals; amulets; crosses. On the floor behind one of the cases was a stuffed border collie mounted on a plank. Mustaine was leaning over the case, taking a closer look at the dog, who seemed happy to be dead, lips stretched into a smile, tail aloft, when a scratchy contralto with no hint of accent asked if he needed help. A trim blonde woman in a white blouse, gray skirt, and a wide black belt had emerged from the office or whatever lay behind the ajar door. Fiftyish; a bit dried-out, but still attractive. Hair elegantly styled. Understated make-up. Faint crow's-feet. Her face was a sexy grandma ad for *Modern Maturity*. He could easily picture her in the offices of a New York publishing house; less easily in a place such as Remedies.

"Just browsing," he said; then, with a measure of guilt: "I was checking out the dog."

"I suppose it's a bit ghoulish, but I wanted to be able to look at her." She stepped behind the case and gave the collie a pat on the head. She glanced at Mustaine. Her eyes were grayish-blue and gave an impression of steadiness. She gestured at the contents of the case. "Would you like to know anything about all this?"

"Yeah, sure. What kinda remedies you got."

"Two kinds, basically. Effective and ineffective." She did not appear to be kidding.

"So," he said, "I guess ineffective remedies aren't your real movers."

"Not at all. I'd say they account for three-quarters of my sales. Many people are defined by their disease. The last thing they want is a cure." Her smile made a brief appearance, as if to suggest that what she had said—while amusing—was nonetheless true.

This was not turning out as Mustaine had expected. He had assumed the shop would be operated by some funky old relic, not Ms. Vassar Class of '72.

"You're not in the market for a remedy, I don't think." The woman produced a pack of Salems from her skirt pocket and tapped one out. "Possibly the shells . . ." She lit up, exhaled a narrow stream of smoke, and stood holding the cigarette to the side, a hand on her hip, as if he were a cover design she was contemplating.

"Nedra!" A pretty black woman wearing a bathrobe, her bronze-colored hair hanging in dozens of thin braids, came out of the back room. The bathrobe was not belted, and she was naked beneath it. She didn't seem self-conscious about the exposure. "You gonna be a while?"

"Fifteen or twenty minutes." The blond woman smiled fondly at her. "Why don't you go upstairs and put on some music?"

With a flirty shrug, shaking her fists in dance moves, the black woman hustled off through the door.

Grail, Louisiana. Kinky Kajunland.

"Would you like me to do a reading?" Nedra asked of Mustaine.

"Uh . . . yeah. How much is it?"

"Twenty-five for a short reading, fifty for the long." She said this pertly, her face composed in a neutral expression.

"Short," Mustaine said.

The back room of Remedies, Nedra said, was also the living room of her apartment, most of which lay upstairs. A sofa of white leather and unfinished cedar. Chairs and coffee table to match. A couple of chrome lamp stands. Grasscloth wallpaper. The Upper West Side transplanted. She asked Mustaine to sit on the sofa and went to a lacquered Chinese cabinet at the far end of the room and removed a leather sack about the size of the pouches full of gold that movie Robin Hoods were always ripping off from fat noblemen back in Sherwood.

"I get the idea you're not from around here," he said as she sat beside him.

"I'm originally from Rhode Island. Newport." She handed him the sack. "But I've lived here for years."

"Grail must be a let-down after Newport."

"How long have you been in town?" she asked.

"Since yesterday."

"Well . . ." She stubbed out her cigarette in an ashtray on the arm of the sofa. "If you stay, perhaps you'll understand. There's a wonderful energy here."

A thumping bass issued from upstairs, penetrating the ceiling. Frowning, Nedra glanced upward, lifted her hand as if signaling a waiter, and closed her eyes. Seconds later, the volume was reduced. Watching this, Mustaine felt like a kid who had fallen into the deep end of the pool and discovered that he could not touch bottom.

"Arlise always forgets how sound carries in this place." Nedra said. She pointed to the sack. "These are cowry shells. They're used for divination. Have you ever worked with them before?"

Mustaine allowed that he had not.

"Are you religious?"

"Not really."

"Very well." She clasped her hands about his, so they were both holding the sack; her fingertips were cool against his wrists. "I want you to concentrate. It's not essential to have a question in mind. Think about something that's important to you."

He bowed his head, picturing Vida's face, the way it looked when she had approached him in Le Bon Chance. Intense. Hungry for life.

Nedra took the sack from him and seemed to be praying. Eyes closed, lips moving. Then she loosened the drawstring and scattered several dozen tiny shells across the surface of the coffee table. They were roughly oval. White with dark speckles and slit openings down the center. Reminiscent of female genitalia. Nedra leaned across the table, holding both hands above the shells. Her nostrils flared and her breathing grew increasingly labored. The shells had spilled into four main groupings, one markedly smaller than the rest. With a practiced movement, she scooped up the shells in the largest grouping and tossed them again onto the table. Studied the new pattern. Then she repeated this process with the remaining groups, her face close to the table, as if she were trying to catch a scent. After about ten minutes, a period during which Mustaine began to feel uneasy, Nedra sighed and sat up straight.

"I usually have a drink after a reading," she said. "Would you care for something?"

"That's it? You're finished?"

"I've completed the divination. Now I have to explain it to you." She stood and smoothed down her skirt. "I have some nice vodka."

"Vodka's fine."

She left the room briefly, returning with two shot glasses of chilled vodka. She lifted her glass to Mustaine and knocked it back. He followed suit.

"You noticed there were four main groups of shells?" She set down her empty glass. "The largest represents your situation in life. The second largest represents you. The third and the fourth groups represent women. One in the recent past, one in the present."

"What about the future?" Mustaine asked, affecting a glibness he did not feel. He was beginning to think she might actually be able to offer him a revelation.

"Anyone who claims they can read the future is a fraud. There is no future, only the present. Even the past is a dream."

Disappointed, he asked, "How does that help? I know all I need to about the present."

Nedra laughed, a single note of mild incredulity. "Really? Tell me, then. How do you see your situation? What's going on with you at the moment?"

He started to speak, but she cut in.

"It's important you're honest with me, no matter how painful that may be."

He told her about LA, his songwriting. "I've got enough money to live for a couple of years . . . but not in LA. I'd piss it away there. So I'm going down to Florida to write. I want to write an album they'll let me record."

"That's not the only reason you left."

"No," he said. "No, I was living with someone. A woman. She was older than me. About your age."

Nedra smiled. "I hesitate to ask how old you think I am."

"You want me to guess?"

She shrugged.

"Forty-eight, forty-nine."

"I'm sixty-one. Please don't tell me I don't look it. I feel every minute of sixty-one." She crossed her legs, straightened the hem of her skirt. "You ran out on this woman. You took something of hers."

"That's one way of putting it."

"Is there a more accurate way?"

He looked down at the speckled profusion of the shells, trying to find himself among them. "No, I guess not."

"Whatever it is," Nedra said, "she can afford it."

"I know." He didn't want to meet her eyes. "It was a strange relationship. I mean, when she came on to me, I thought it was strange. But I really liked her . . ."

"You liked her, but you also were aware that she could help your career, and you can't reconcile that. You suspect you were only using her." Nedra leaned forward and took his right hand. "But you weren't. You liked her, though not as much as she liked you. That was dishonest, but no more so than most of us."

Mustaine realized that though her fingers were extremely cold, his hand was growing warmer, as if whatever warmth she possessed was flowing into him.

"You need to take care of this," she said. "Call her. Explain that she was mothering you, and that was difficult for you. Admit your weakness and things will go well."

"I thought you couldn't read the future."

"This has nothing whatsoever to do with clairvoyance. I can read you, I can read the woman. Certain things become apparent."

"It was a car," Mustaine said after a silence. "She bought it for me. My old car died and she wanted to surprise me. Couple of days after she gave it to me, I was supposed to do some session work. I threw my guitars in the trunk, and instead of heading to the studio I started driving east. I kept thinking I was going to turn around."

"It was your car," Nedra said.

"Yeah, but . . . I'm supposed to pay her back."

Nedra made an "oh well" noise. "You'll have to deal with it. Right now you have more immediate worries."

Mustaine looked at her expectantly.

"The second woman," she said. "Tell me about her."

"I've only known her a little while, but I've fallen in love with her. She's got some problems."

Nedra formed a church-and-steeple with her fingers. "Her problems are not mental."

"I don't know about that. She's pretty messed up."

"Not in the way you suppose. She's at the center of two opposing magical forces . . . each trying to claim her for its own. It's taken an enormous act of will on her part to distance herself from one of these forces. Now she's in danger from the other."

Mustaine was distracted by the sight of the black woman, Arlise, peeking at them from the doorway that led to the upstairs.

"Did you hear what I said?" Nedra asked.

"Uh-huh. But I . . ."

"I realize you don't believe in magic, but you'd better learn to suspend your disbelief if you want things to work out between you." Nedra leaned toward him. "Do you think life is so simple it can be explained by a single philosophical system? This woman you love, she may well be having psychological problems; but they're the result of magical operations. There are any number of reasons why any one thing happens. They're congruent, those reasons—they flow together, even though they often appear to run contrary to each other. You can't examine just one and hope to make sense of the world. You have to accept that this woman is the object of a magical struggle. You have to understand that you are not only her lover, but also a figure in that struggle. That's who she perceives you to be . . . as someone who embodies a force that can save her. And according to the shells, that's who you are."

When Mustaine failed to respond she asked if he understood, and he said, "Hell, no!"

"What is it you don't understand?"

He was inclined to say that he didn't understand why he had paid twenty-five dollars to see her show. What happens for fifty bucks? he wanted to ask. You get topless before you start sniffing the shells? Yet he could not quite convince himself that she was hustling him. Though the thought that he might be the embodiment of some potent salvation was patently absurd, though aware that this sort of intimation was a staple in the canon of every tent show psychic and fortune teller, he was tempted to buy into it if only for the reason that Vida clearly needed saving and he had been the one to happen along. But more than that, the concept of congruent explanations for every worldly event, a concept he would previously have decried as being ludicrous . . . it seemed plausible now that everything was true, every apparent opposition a form of congruency. Perhaps the force that had joined itself to him was allowing him to see more deeply into the veil of illusion. Yet at the same time he wondered how he could entertain the notion. It went contrary to everything he understood about the world. But maybe this was only another instance of congruency.

"You're telling me," he said, "I have to believe everything she says?"

"It's not necessary. But it would help her cause—and

yours—if you stopped regarding what she tells you as part of a mental failure and kept an open mind."

"I don't know." Mustaine ran a hand through his hair. "She's talking some crazy shit. Witch men from New Orleans sending her visions. Using shadows to perform proxy rapes. She says this witch man kept her in his house and handed her out like a party favor to his pals. She . . ."

Mustaine broke off, seeing that Nedra's face had hardened.

"This woman," she said. "Is her name Vida Dumars?"

"You must have heard this before, huh? Yeah, it's her. Maybe you can . . ."

Nedra got to her feet. "I have an appointment. I'm afraid you'll have to go. I'm sorry."

Mustaine, too, stood. "What's going on?"

"I told you . . . I have an appointment." She gestured toward the door, inviting him to precede her.

"Y'know," he said, "seems the second you realized I was talking about Vida your whole attitude changed."

"Not at all. I simply remembered an appointment. If you wish to return another day, that's fine."

She ushered him through the shop and out the door and closed it firmly behind him. Blinking against the sunlight, a bit disoriented, Mustaine realized that in her haste she had not bothered to collect his twenty-five dollars. He stood for a couple of seconds, getting his bearings, then started west up Monroe; but as he reached the corner of the building, a woman called to him: "Hey, Mister!"

It was Arlise, holding her bathrobe closed about her breasts. She peered at him through the beaded curtain of her braids and said, "You wanna help Vida, drive out past the road leads to her place. 'Bout a quarter-mile. There's a path leads back into the swamp. You follow it to a shanty set on the water, you gon' find somethin'll explain what's happenin' to Vida."

She retreated toward the rear of the building and Mustaine said, "Hey, I want to talk to you!"

"I got to get back!"

"Why would you help me?" he asked, suddenly suspicious.

"Vida's my friend. She baby-sit me when I was little. You help her, I'll help you." She backed away, heels scuffing up puffs of yellow dust. "Best you can do is get her away from this damn place!"

10

The Hour of Prayer

*A*T THE REAR OF VIDA'S MOONLIGHT DINER, UNDER the shade of the overhang, facing a thicket of chokecherry, mixed in with shrimp plants and chicory bushes, was a rusting metal lawn chair that showed traces of its original turquoise paint. It was there that Vida sat after the lunch crowd had thinned, taking a break. Ordinarily she might have read a paperback or smoked a cigarette—she was down to a pack a week. But on this occasion she prayed to be free of Clifford Marsh. Vida was a non-discriminatory supplicant. She prayed to Jesus Christ and the Virgin Mary; to Shango and Erzulie, the god and goddess who had inspirited her parents' bodies on the night she was conceived. She prayed as well to Metabalon, a god introduced to her by a street preacher in New Orleans; to Kotay Zaizul, a shapeshifting goddess worshipped by members of a storefront church in Algiers; and to a dozen other deities whom she had brushed against during her sojourn in the Big Easy. But mostly she prayed to the Great Cloud of Being, which was still circling over the town and thus within certain hailing distance. In

large part her prayer was wordless, a beam of hope and yearning. But every so often she would whisper the name Zedaial
and address herself to the Form whose name it was.

"Listen, you," she said. "I know you listenin', so you keep
on tellin' me what to do. I don't understand what it is you
need from me, but you make it plain, I'll do it, me."

The pendulous pink blossoms of a shrimp plant trembled
in a breeze; the blooms had been transformed into two-inch-
long erect phalluses, quivering with arousal.

"Can't you do somethin'?" she went on. "Somethin'll stop
that man from tormentin' me?"

The wind picked up, stirring the crowns of the trees
beyond the thicket, and she could have sworn she heard a
windy word shaped from the limbs and leaves: "Eeeasst. . . ."

"East?" she said. "You want me to go east? Fine. I'll go
east. But that don't help me now."

The tops of the thicket shivered, thousands of spiky leaves
changing into wicked-looking dark green men with pointy
hats. In their eyes were the even tinier shapes of coiled
serpents, and in the eyes of the serpents were shapes too small
for her to distinguish. She understood the Form was remind-
ing her of the multiplicity of forms, the infinite levels. Marsh
only controlled one level, and she needed to look past it, to
find a place where she could rest her eyes and be untroubled.
For a moment it seemed to help. The leafy faces of the men
dissolved into images of the Virgin and she whispered a Hail
Mary in gratitude.

But Marsh, as always, outfoxed her.

From the faint clatter in the kitchen, the squeak and whir
of the ventilator fan, the chatter of Anson's radio tuned to an
all-talk station, from those and a multitude of lesser sounds,
Marsh cooked up a conversation. Many voices. A babble like
that of a crowded party. Probably one of his special afternoons
taking place that very moment. She could hear each voice
particularly, and they were all scandalizing her. That Vida,
said a man, she ain't nothin' but two hips and a hole. Then a
refined male voice, sandy and soft, like a whisper with the

the tables of buzzcut khaki-clad drunken GIs, and the Tu Do cowboy-types standing around in small groups, arms folded, stern, too cool for this rowdy, stupid, American heat. The illusion started to act upon Mustaine. Outside were sappers, jungles, and 'villes, not rednecks, swamps, and hick towns. Now and then an explosion, a rocket shrieking overhead. He found a way to integrate these things into the music he had stumbled upon at Le Bon Chance. Employing fewer notes, generating feedback to punch holes in the melody.

The breakdown was more impressionistic this time around, illustrating the mystical sickness of Grail, the brain damage of the night. He felt the guitar was channeling the music from some wiser head, the patterns of notes illuminating the invisible patterns that ruled not only the town, but the world that contained it, the ones that prevented you from realizing dreams, from achieving the smallest transcendence, yet that also protected you from the dangers of transcendence, thereby enforcing a neurotic security, a mediocrity glorious for its stability . . . People were standing and cheering. He supposed it was for the music. Then he saw Vida dancing on stage among the bar girls. Not mimicking their disinterested style. Her dance was all heat and vigor. Like she was working out a violent impulse in 4/4 time. If it had been another night, another woman who had jumped on the stage, he would have played to the moment. He would have moved close and made her twitch faster. But Vida disrupted his focus. Her abandon seemed to have less to do with the music than with derangement, and the crowd's gleeful approval brought home the perversity of their circumstance. He unstrapped the guitar and the rhythm fell apart behind him; the bar girls quit dancing. Vida staggered as if she'd been shot. He crossed the stage, brushing past the bar girls who, with passive-aggressive languor, put themselves in his path, and caught Vida by the waist. She tried to pull away. She blinked, appearing to recognize him, but reacted dazedly. How, he wondered, could she have gotten drunk so fast? Then he realized he had left her alone for almost an hour.

"I want to dance some more," she said, looping her arms about his neck. "Dance with me."

"We can dance outside. Let's go."

As he walked her down off the stage, the band struck up an amateurish version of "Sympathy for the Devil" that, with its lurching, fragmented ineptitude and whined vocals, felt more truly demonic than the original.

"Oh, I love that song!" Vida pushed at his chest, closed her fists and swayed unsteadily, unable to catch the rhythm. "Come on, Jack! Please!"

"Nobody can dance to that shit," said Mustaine, though behind them everybody was dancing.

Drunk, but not so drunk as she had been, Vida sat on the curb with Jack beside her, his arm around her waist. She wished she hadn't done all those shooters with John Guineau and his friends. She hadn't had a drink for years, afraid that drunkenness would lower her defenses against Marsh. But knowing he was gone, she had wanted to celebrate her freedom. She still felt like dancing. Sitting there was like sitting in a comfortably warm flame made of Jack and tequila, but she wanted to move, to liberate herself from the vestiges of woe. The Form had done its promised work. She was one answered prayer closer to the mainline of life, and once she got away from Grail, once she settled on the shores of a different ocean, New Smyrna, and God! What would that be like. . . ? Once she got away from Grail, even if Marsh regained his strength, she would be beyond him.

She bumped Jack with her shoulder, trying to rouse a smile. He just sat there like a crooked black stick turned into a man, brooding over something . . . she didn't care what. She'd put a smile on his face before the night was through. She looked off along the street. The mist had thickened; it was getting downright hard to see and almost everybody was inside one or another of the bars. The only people in sight were a handful of Joe Dill's Vietnamese. Some boys with motor scooters, old women, a slim coppery-colored man in shorts sitting cross-legged across the way, repairing a bicycle that was propped upside down in front of him. Vida liked it better where she was crowned Queen. Out on Beauford Monroe's estate. Sedele's daddy. That night had been misty same as this. Beauford had set metal torches everywhere outside and they had gleamed like foxfire in the misty dark. Here, with all these bright electric lights, it wouldn't half be so pretty.

"How long's it all going to take," Jack asked. "This coronation deal."

"Half-hour, maybe. Little more." She caressed his hair. "Don't act so put upon! You might enjoy it."

"I doubt it."

"You might! For me, most of the fun is tryin' to guess how they choose the queen."

"Don't they just vote . . . or have judges?"

"Oh, no! See it's gotta be like the Good Gray Man does the choosin'. So they let him speak through somethin' of nature."

He flashed her a quizzical look.

"My year, they did the choosin' with a serpent. They dragged a big ol' blacksnake outa the swamp, and whichever of us it wriggled up to, she'd be the queen."

"I woulda wriggled up to you . . . it'd been me."

"You ain't no snake." She leaned her head back into his shoulder. " 'Cept sometimes."

The mist was growing thicker, stained into zones of hazy color by the neon and the lights from inside the bars, and Vida thought maybe it would be a pretty coronation after all, the little girls in their white dresses walking through gauzy scarves of lavender and green and rose.

" 'Course there was some controversy when I was chosen," she said. "I musta stepped on somethin', some dead critter, and got blood on my shoe. So when the snake come to me, some said it was 'cause it smelled the blood on my shoe and they accused my mama of puttin' it there. Which was a lie. There was dogs everywhere 'round the place where I was chosen. They're always killin' squirrels . . . cats. Probably I stepped in some ol' piece of a barn cat."

Something was bothering Jack again, his mouth was all tight and unsmiling. Vida caught his chin in her bunched fingers and shook him gently. "I wish you'd relax! Won't be long 'fore we outa here and headin' east. We can drive a couple hours, then get us a motel."

"I was thinking we'd drive straight through," he said.

"No . . . un-unh. Nosir! We don't wanna do that. What you need to do is drive us to Biloxi and find us a room at the nicest motel in town."

He was smiling now. "That's how you see things going, huh? Things'll work out best we do it your way?"

"Oh, yeah," she said. "I promise!"

Mustaine couldn't recall whether he'd had any expectation of the coronation, other than that it would be cheesy, stupid, a drag. He could not have predicted it would have any effect on him except, perhaps, to increase his impatience to be gone. But from the outset he felt an occult menace, an impression he tried unsuccessfully to rationalize in terms of his having overdosed on the weirdness of Grail. More than a thousand people lined the misted street, talking murmurously, like a crowd awaiting the opening of theater doors. No music could be heard. Acting the part of an army officer, dressed in fatigues—jacket, cap, pants—Joe Dill paced about at the center of the street, occasionally speaking into a walkie-talkie and receiving static-garbled replies. A good many of his Vietnamese bit-actors had removed themselves from the scene and were leaning out upstairs windows. Vida was standing in front of the yellow church, holding a club of twisted dark wood as if it were a bouquet, looking relatively self-possessed, and Mustaine had secured a position thirty feet down from her, in among people he hadn't previously met, though several of them smiled and said hello. Their simple village friendliness, so untypical of the town, heightened his anxiety. Then Joe Dill waved his arm, retreated back into the crowd, and all the talking stopped. Everything was muffled. Heartbeat-quiet. Just stirrings. The mist thinned and thickened

The shanty had the look of a structure that had been dropped from a low height and as a result was collapsing inward, its gray weathered planks warped to form walls with shallow concavities, and its tarpaper roof sagging. The windows were covered by sheets of soggy cardboard and the three steps that led up to the door were bowed and cracked. The door hung one-hinged. Yet there was an air of habitation about the place. Mustaine called out to whoever might be within. The rain fell harder, cold and drenching. He called out again and when he received no reply, he went cautiously up the steps and pushed in through the door. A reeking darkness rolled over him, a sickly sweet odor of human decay. In the dim light he saw a bed—a nest, really—constructed of heaped moldering blankets and grimy pillows and various other cloth relics that might have been sheets or garments. A wood stove dominated the rear wall and opposite the bed stood a poorly carpentered table and chair. Resting on the table were several newspapers, mildewed paperbacks, and a scrapbook with a red binding. Dishes and pots were stacked on the stove, and the floor was carpeted with scraps of cellophane, candy wrappers, rags, cardboard, and such.

The rain intensified, seething on the tarpaper roof, big drops splattering off the steps. Mustaine sat gingerly in the chair, wary of its creaking. He stared out at the cypresses, curtained now by the rain, and at the repetitive perspectives they offered of more trees, more black water, wondering who would choose to live in such a dismal place. Before long he turned his attention to the table, picked up a paperback. It was entitled *Moon Dreams: An Astrological Guide to the World of Your Dreams*. All the paperbacks, he discovered, dealt with the subject of dreams and their interpretation. He recalled Vida's books and thought it odd, the similarity between the two collections. The scrapbook was a record of newsworthy events in the life of one Madeleine LeCleuse, all the clippings bearing the banner of the *Grail Seeker*. On the first page was a birth notice and an accompanying photograph showing the infant Madeleine with proud parents John and Nora. Next was an article about a ballet class winning some regional competition—Madeleine had earned an individual award. He flipped past several pages, then stopped, his eye drawn by a headline:

MADELEINE LECLEUSE CHOSEN
MIDSUMMER QUEEN

The dateline of the article was forty years previously. To the day. A photograph showed a pretty prepubescent girl, mature for her age, dressed like a princess in a white gown with a bell skirt and lots of chiffon. On her head, nestled among black curls, was a tiara, and cradled in her left arm was the parody of a bouquet, gathered weeds and withered flowers. A clublike length of cypress root served as her scepter.

This second similarity between Madeleine and Vida unnerved Mustaine. He skimmed the rest of the pages. For twenty years after being selected Midsummer Queen, Madeleine had lived an ordinary, moderately successful life. Marriage, but no children. A real-estate sales award. Church activities. The death of her husband in a boating accident. Fund-raising for a Democratic congressional candidate. Elected to the parish board. Then, twenty years after she had been anointed Midsummer Queen, she presented the bouquet and tiara to her successor, Vida Dumars. In the photograph, Vida's hair fell to her butt and her figure was as straight as a stick; but Mustaine could see the woman in the child. Madeleine, who had grown into a beautiful woman, looked aggrieved.

There were no further clippings, only a picture drawn in gray crayon loose between the next two pages, depicting a featureless anthropomorphic figure.

A gray shadow.

The symmetries, implied and overt, between the two women's lives provoked Mustaine to imagine that they might also share a symmetry of fate, but he dismissed this as fantasy. He did not even know whether the occupant of the cabin was

Madeleine herself or a relative . . . perhaps an old friend. But Arlise said that he would find something to explain what was happening to Vida.

What else could it be?

The rain stopped abruptly, but the overcast held. Mustaine reread several of the clippings, but could glean no more pertinent information. A mist was forming close above the water, gradually creating a carpeting like a lumpy field of dirty snow from which the bleached trunks of the cypresses appeared to sprout. All the sounds of the place had subsided. He considered going back to town, but thought there must be something else in the cabin that would shed light on the situation. He poked at the bed, examined the cans on the shelves beside the stove, kicked the litter around. Giving up on a search, he turned yet again to the scrapbook, studying the clippings he had skipped.

The light dimmed. Dimmed as suddenly as the rain had stopped. Startled, Mustaine looked to the door. A ragged figure stood silhouetted on the top step. He jumped to his feet, expecting an angry confrontation, but the figure neither spoke nor gestured, and after a moment, as if accustomed to such invasions of privacy, she shuffled into the cabin and removed a can of soup from inside her shapeless robe and set it on a shelf. She was heavier by far than the images of Madeleine he had seen in the clippings. Her gray hair stuck out like jackstraws, matted about her shoulders; her sagging face, what he could see of it, was seamed and ravaged, betraying no sign of the woman she had been. It seemed the room was darker for her presence, that she had dragged in a pall of fresh shadow.

"Madeleine LeCleuse?" he said.

She crossed to the bed and collapsed upon it with a sigh. "I coulda swore you was him for a second," she said. "Best you run along. He be finishin' up with me tonight, him."

Her voice, a dry whisper, stirred a rustling from a darkened corner, as if she and her home were in decaying resonance with one another.

"I'm a friend of Vida Dumars," Mustaine said.

"That poor thing. She ain't nothin' but ice cream for the Devil." She made a whimpering noise that, after it kept up for several seconds, he recognized to be humming.

"Why's she a poor thing?"

She shifted about on the nest of blankets. "What you talking at me for, boy? I want to eat my soup and pray."

He decided to try a different tack. "Who you pray to?"

She snuffled, wiped her nose on her collar; her eyes glinted behind the hatchings of hair. "You a Christian boy? You want to convert me?" She grunted. "You too damn late for that."

"I just want to know."

Something—a bird, perhaps—shrieked from out in the swamp. Mustaine repeated his question.

"I be prayin' to most everything these days. Le Gros Bon Ange, He everywhere, Him." She spat out a noise that he took for a laugh. "Le Gris Bon Ange . . . Him, too."

He started to ask another question, but she was muttering to herself, speaking in a language composed of harsh glottals and chuckling half-swallowed vowels. For a scrap of time he felt her presence intensely, as a man trapped beneath a massive stone would feel—dazed, distant from pain, but sensing a terrible pressure close at hand. Fear crawled inside him. Not the this-shit-isn't-happening kind he'd experienced when the cop had hassled him, but a wormy, gut-coiling fear of something on the very edge of his perceptions, something dogs might see but he could not. He tried another question: "What's going to happen to Vida Dumars?"

The pace of labored, glutinous breathing increased. "Oh, he gon' come to her tryin' to get his body born. He gon' come to her every night, him."

"You mean Marsh? That who you talking about?"

"That his name . . . Marsh?" she asked. "You know him, too?"

"I've heard about him."

"Marsh be a good name for that one." More humming, then she said, "He gon' come extra hard to Vida."

volume turned high, Marsh's voice . . . it said, Don't be getting on Vida. She runs a lot deeper than that. Oh, yeah, another man said. She's deep all right. She's so deep, I hit her G-spot once and my dick come back speaking Chinese. That, too, drew a laugh, followed by a round of similar jokes. But Marsh's voice compelled the others to silence. Poor Vida, he said. Sitting there all alone. The Midsummer Queen on her rusty throne. The sweetest cooze in Louisianne going dried up and dismal. Your body's born to bestow blessing and your mind's been schooled to passion. You can't live with just one bullfrog humped on your lily pad, sweet Vida. You're fooling yourself to think you can fly away and be a nice little wife to this loser car thief you've taken up with. There's too much juice in you. You've got to let loose. You . . .

"He's not a car thief!" she said. "He's the gift of Zedaial. He's . . ."

Same difference, Marsh said. Whatever he is, he's not enough for you. Come back to us. Vida. We'll love you 'til you die . . .

"Why you want me so bad?" she shouted. "What is it? Tell me!"

But he never would. And maybe, she thought, he didn't know himself. Maybe his masters were using them both for their own purposes.

There are many reasons, Vida, he said. Some I can see and some I can't. The web we're woven into has so many strands, we can't know them all. If I picked only one, you'd misunderstand me.

"Liar!" she said. "You lie . . . you always lie!"

Listen to me, he said, and a host of sibilant voices at his back chorused, Listen . . .

She sat up straight, conditioned to obey him.

You're crumbling, he said. Breaking down. Grail is breaking down. They think you can save them, they think you can ground the charge that's killing them. The charge their daddies loosed when they made their bargain with the Good Gray Man. Maybe you can save them for a while. But the end

is coming. That little island of insanity's going to be swallowed up again by the chaos that spawned it. You want to be
part of that? You will be if you stay. You know what happens
to the Midsummer Queen. . . .

"I *don't* know! You keep sayin' I do, but I don't know!"

It's not my place to tell you, but the answer's right in front
of your face. . . .

One of the chokecherry bushes had taken on the shape of
a leafy vulva, its lips parted to reveal a turbulent dark depth.
Within that depth Vida saw herself . . . yet not herself.
Misshapen, somehow. She couldn't quite make the figure
out, but nonetheless it terrified her. The way it stumbled
onward, clumsy and aimless.

Last chance, Vida . . .

"Stop!" she cried. "Please . . . Jesus! Stop!"

His voice grew fainter, more wind than word, and she had
to fill in the gaps where the voice wisped out.

I can't ho-o-o-ld out against hiiiiim, Viiiida. He's too straw-
aw-awng. Laaaaaast chaaaaaaaaance . . .

She bent her head, pressed the heels of her hands to her
ears, stoppering them against Marsh's voice, and prayed
harder than ever to all the gods previously cited and a few
more she'd forgotten the first time. She couldn't feel her body
and wondered if her hair was on fire, tresses flying up in the
puffs of wind generated by their own burning. Her eyes grew
cold as if covered with silver coins. Her lips, she thought,
were bleeding. Sliced by the desperately hissed words
"please" and "Jesus."

A hand fell to her shoulder and she stiffened.

Vida heard a voice call her name.

She glanced up and saw Anson, blotting his sweaty brow
with the back of his arm. His white T-shirt stained with beef
blood.

"Girl, you okay?" he asked.

"Oh no, Anson," she said. "I ain't okay." She brushed a
wisp of hair from her eyes, and the gesture seemed to weaken
her, to take the last of her good energy. "What's wrong?"

"We gettin' us a crowd," he told her. "Buncha folks up from Shreveport for St. John's Eve. Must be a shortage of food over there in Shreveport. They orderin' everything on the damn menu. I can't handle it my own self."

"God!" Vida put her head down again.

"I know you poorly, but I can't handle it."

She struggled to her feet, as slow and ungainly as the figure in the vision that might have been herself. Feeling too heavy to live.

Anson paused in the doorway and looked back at her. "You comin', girl?"

"Just ease your egg bag. I'll be along directly," Vida said.

11

The Moment of Truth

*T*HE PATH TO WHICH ARLISE HAD DIRECTED MUSTAINE was choked with wild indigo and ferns, and led him into a deep green shade. Slants of pale dust-hung light touched the tops of the bushes. Overhead, grackles and jays racketed in the oak crowns; crickets chirred, and frogs loosed a medley of throaty bubbling noises that taken altogether had the sound of an electronically simulated drizzle. The air was thick with the smells of dampness and rot. Whenever Mustaine pushed aside a branch, his arm was drenched with dew from the leaves. After a few minutes he caught sight of a shanty on a point of land extending out into the black water of a cypress swamp, the great trees standing forth like the ruined pillars of a fallen palace whose roof once had spanned miles. Gray clouds were moving in from the Gulf and by the time Mustaine had picked his way through the thickets guarding the point, an overcast had sealed off the sky and wind was driving ripples across the water, swaying the beards of moss on the cypress boughs. Drops of rain produced numb circles on his skin. The temperature was dropping rapidly.

The shanty had the look of a structure that had been dropped from a low height and as a result was collapsing inward, its gray weathered planks warped to form walls with shallow concavities, and its tarpaper roof sagging. The windows were covered by sheets of soggy cardboard and the three steps that led up to the door were bowed and cracked. The door hung one-hinged. Yet there was an air of habitation about the place. Mustaine called out to whoever might be within. The rain fell harder, cold and drenching. He called out again and when he received no reply, he went cautiously up the steps and pushed in through the door. A reeking darkness rolled over him, a sickly sweet odor of human decay. In the dim light he saw a bed—a nest, really—constructed of heaped moldering blankets and grimy pillows and various other cloth relics that might have been sheets or garments. A wood stove dominated the rear wall and opposite the bed stood a poorly carpentered table and chair. Resting on the table were several newspapers, mildewed paperbacks, and a scrapbook with a red binding. Dishes and pots were stacked on the stove, and the floor was carpeted with scraps of cellophane, candy wrappers, rags, cardboard, and such.

The rain intensified, seething on the tarpaper roof, big drops splattering off the steps. Mustaine sat gingerly in the chair, wary of its creaking. He stared out at the cypresses, curtained now by the rain, and at the repetitive perspectives they offered of more trees, more black water, wondering who would choose to live in such a dismal place. Before long he turned his attention to the table, picked up a paperback. It was entitled *Moon Dreams: An Astrological Guide to the World of Your Dreams*. All the paperbacks, he discovered, dealt with the subject of dreams and their interpretation. He recalled Vida's books and thought it odd, the similarity between the two collections. The scrapbook was a record of newsworthy events in the life of one Madeleine LeCleuse, all the clippings bearing the banner of the *Grail Seeker*. On the first page was a birth notice and an accompanying photograph showing the infant Madeleine with proud parents John and Nora. Next was an article about a ballet class winning some regional competition—Madeleine had earned an individual award. He flipped past several pages, then stopped, his eye drawn by a headline:

MADELEINE LeCLEUSE CHOSEN
MIDSUMMER QUEEN

The dateline of the article was forty years previously. To the day. A photograph showed a pretty prepubescent girl, mature for her age, dressed like a princess in a white gown with a bell skirt and lots of chiffon. On her head, nestled among black curls, was a tiara, and cradled in her left arm was the parody of a bouquet, gathered weeds and withered flowers. A clublike length of cypress root served as her scepter.

This second similarity between Madeleine and Vida unnerved Mustaine. He skimmed the rest of the pages. For twenty years after being selected Midsummer Queen, Madeleine had lived an ordinary, moderately successful life. Marriage, but no children. A real-estate sales award. Church activities. The death of her husband in a boating accident. Fund-raising for a Democratic congressional candidate. Elected to the parish board. Then, twenty years after she had been anointed Midsummer Queen, she presented the bouquet and tiara to her successor, Vida Dumars. In the photograph, Vida's hair fell to her butt and her figure was as straight as a stick; but Mustaine could see the woman in the child. Madeleine, who had grown into a beautiful woman, looked aggrieved.

There were no further clippings, only a picture drawn in gray crayon loose between the next two pages, depicting a featureless anthropomorphic figure.

A gray shadow.

The symmetries, implied and overt, between the two women's lives provoked Mustaine to imagine that they might also share a symmetry of fate, but he dismissed this as fantasy. He did not even know whether the occupant of the cabin was

Madeleine herself or a relative . . . perhaps an old friend. But
Arlise said that he would find something to explain what was
happening to Vida.

What else could it be?

The rain stopped abruptly, but the overcast held.
Mustaine reread several of the clippings, but could glean no
more pertinent information. A mist was forming close above
the water, gradually creating a carpeting like a lumpy field of
dirty snow from which the bleached trunks of the cypresses
appeared to sprout. All the sounds of the place had subsided.
He considered going back to town, but thought there must be
something else in the cabin that would shed light on the situation. He poked at the bed, examined the cans on the shelves
beside the stove, kicked the litter around. Giving up on a
search, he turned yet again to the scrapbook, studying the
clippings he had skipped.

The light dimmed. Dimmed as suddenly as the rain had
stopped. Startled, Mustaine looked to the door. A ragged
figure stood silhouetted on the top step. He jumped to his
feet, expecting an angry confrontation, but the figure neither
spoke nor gestured, and after a moment, as if accustomed to
such invasions of privacy, she shuffled into the cabin and
removed a can of soup from inside her shapeless robe and set
it on a shelf. She was heavier by far than the images of
Madeleine he had seen in the clippings. Her gray hair stuck
out like jackstraws, matted about her shoulders; her sagging
face, what he could see of it, was seamed and ravaged, betraying no sign of the woman she had been. It seemed the room
was darker for her presence, that she had dragged in a pall of
fresh shadow.

"Madeleine LeCleuse?" he said.

She crossed to the bed and collapsed upon it with a sigh.
"I coulda swore you was him for a second," she said. "Best you
run along. He be finishin' up with me tonight, him."

Her voice, a dry whisper, stirred a rustling from a darkened
corner, as if she and her home were in decaying resonance
with one another.

"I'm a friend of Vida Dumars," Mustaine said.

"That poor thing. She ain't nothin' but ice cream for the Devil." She made a whimpering noise that, after it kept up for several seconds, he recognized to be humming.

"Why's she a poor thing?"

She shifted about on the nest of blankets. "What you talking at me for, boy? I want to eat my soup and pray."

He decided to try a different tack. "Who you pray to?"

She snuffled, wiped her nose on her collar; her eyes glinted behind the hatchings of hair. "You a Christian boy? You want to convert me?" She grunted. "You too damn late for that."

"I just want to know."

Something—a bird, perhaps—shrieked from out in the swamp. Mustaine repeated his question.

"I be prayin' to most everything these days. Le Gros Bon Ange, He everywhere, Him." She spat out a noise that he took for a laugh. "Le Gris Bon Ange . . . Him, too."

He started to ask another question, but she was muttering to herself, speaking in a language composed of harsh glottals and chuckling half-swallowed vowels. For a scrap of time he felt her presence intensely, as a man trapped beneath a massive stone would feel—dazed, distant from pain, but sensing a terrible pressure close at hand. Fear crawled inside him. Not the this-shit-isn't-happening kind he'd experienced when the cop had hassled him, but a wormy, gut-coiling fear of something on the very edge of his perceptions, something dogs might see but he could not. He tried another question: "What's going to happen to Vida Dumars?"

The pace of labored, glutinous breathing increased. "Oh, he gon' come to her tryin' to get his body born. He gon' come to her every night, him."

"You mean Marsh? That who you talking about?"

"That his name . . . Marsh?" she asked. "You know him, too?"

"I've heard about him."

"Marsh be a good name for that one." More humming, then she said, "He gon' come extra hard to Vida."

"What do you mean?"

She gave a sigh that was almost a moan. "You must not know him, boy. Else you never be askin' that. Now leave me be. I need to do my prayin' 'fore he comes."

After that she spoke no more, though Mustaine continued to question her a while longer. The mist was becoming a problem, thick and swirling, sending tendrils through the shanty door, and finally, fearful that he might lose his way on the path, he left Madeleine to her muttering, her soup, her prayers, and started back toward the road. Except for the sounds of water dripping, the place was silent; but his footsteps seemed abnormally loud as he squashed matted leaves and sodden twigs into the mucky ground. He felt a little out of breath, as if the air—polluted by the mist—was not quite right; he could barely see a yard in any direction. Branches overhanging the path materialized from the gray to pluck wetly at his sleeves and chest. But as he churned up an incline, about a quarter mile from where he'd left Vida's pickup, an aperture formed in the mist to his right and he thought he saw a figure standing twenty-five or thirty feet from the path. Large and roughly human in shape. Featureless. It could have been a shadow, one a slightly darker gray than its surround.

In the instant before the aperture closed, Mustaine had the impression he was being watched, that the figure was observing him, taking specific notice. The notion that he might be known to this specter overrode his natural tendency toward disbelief, nourishing the germ of fear that had infected him at the shanty. He pressed faster through the brush, restrained from running by his lack of familiarity with the terrain, and when he caught sight of breaks between the trees, the pale light of uncanopied air and the dark bulk of the pickup looming on the shoulder, then he did run, digging for the highway, his heart seeming to ride higher and hotter in his chest. He threw himself into the passenger side, locked both doors and sat with his head down on the steering wheel until his pulse slowed and his breath had steamed the windows.

"This place," he said, just to hear a voice, "is seriously fucking me up."

He rested his head against the door and had a Creature Feature moment, imagining an enormous elephant-colored hand splayed across the windshield. He switched on the ignition, gunned the engine, and sent the pickup rolling toward Grail, keeping it under twenty because of the mist. He pictured the gray figure gripping the tailgate, being dragged along, hauling itself up onto the bed. He dismissed the image and tried to align all the similarities between Madeleine and Vida, to create a coherent structure of them, one that would allow him to determine exactly what was wrong and what might be done; but it was as if the materials of the past hours were themselves made of mist, swirling and ungraspable. He felt rattled. Like a loose shutter was banging back and forth in his brain. He had no need to inquire of Nedra Hawes for a remedy. A cocktail was definitely required.

12

Happy Hour

*A*T QUARTER TO FOUR LE BON CHANCE WAS QUIET AND dim and all but empty. A couple of farmers in jeans and baseball caps were playing pinochle at a corner table, and nearby a pear-shaped white woman in a green coverall was lazily pushing a mop across what might have been a blood-stain. An old man wearing a seersucker suit nursed a beer at one end of the bar; at the opposite end, Sedele, Nedra, and Arlise were drinking Cryptoverdes. Earl the bartender, a skinny glum Elvis impersonator, was rinsing off glassware. When he spotted Mustaine he adopted an inquiring look and held up a Cryptoverde glass.

"Jack Black double and a beer back," said Mustaine, stationing himself midway between the women and the old man. Once Earl had poured, Mustaine threw down the double and ordered another. The bite of the whiskey steadied him, but he was still flustered. Sedele peered at him over Nedra's shoulder. He blew her a mean-spirited kiss and felt better.

"Gettin' us a little weather today," Earl said, refilling his glass. "But it'll clear off by tonight. It don't never rain on St. John's Eve."

Earl went back to rinsing and shortly thereafter Arlise came up and sat beside him, Faded jeans, a light brown Tipatina's T-shirt, and a gold bracelet whose antique delicacy seemed more redolent of old-money Newport than of Grail.

A psychic love gift, Mustaine figured.

"Nedra ast' me to be friendly with you," Arlise said, shaking back braids from her face, "so's I can find out what you know."

"What I know." Mustaine had a swallow of beer. "Yeah."

"You go to the swamp like I told you?"

He nodded. "Uh-huh. I had big fun."

She studied him, then put a hand to her mouth in apparent alarm. "You saw him!"

"Saw who?"

"The Good Gray Man. Don't tell me you didn't! I'm readin' it in your face."

"Is everybody in this goddamn town a psychic?"

" 'Bout everybody born here is," she said. "Though I been told ol' Miz Gammage over at the Smart Mart done lost the power. And Vida, she been away so long, her gift whittled away some."

He waited for her to declare what she had said to be a joke, but she continued to study him.

"I know you seen him," she said. "And he seen you."

"I saw something. Or maybe I didn't. Might have been a tree."

"Tree put no marks on a person like the ones you carryin'."

Mustaine recalled what Vida had said about the Good Gray Man. How he had guaranteed luck for the town in exchange for . . . what had she said? So long as they kept the tradition of the Midsummer Queen? He thought of the figure he'd seen. The drawing in Madeleine's scrapbook. It was possible, he supposed, to accept that the Good Gray Man was an ancient spirit who used the various Midsummer Queens for its own purposes. But he wasn't ready to buy it. Not on the basis of a local legend, a crayon drawing, and a shaky moment in the mist.

"What you know about the Good Gray Man?" he asked Arlise.

"You the one seen him." She flipped her braids to the side and looked at her reflection in the mirror behind the bar; she practiced a smile.

"I thought you were on my side . . . Vida's side."

"I can't tell you what I don't know. Some say he's a spirit 'scaped from Hell. Some say he used to be a man and he's lookin' for his lost love." Still gazing into the mirror, she tried a pouty look and appeared pleased with the result.

Sedele and Nedra were staring daggers at Mustaine.

"What's up with them?" he asked.

"They know you been to the swamp," Arlise said.

"Did you tell them?"

"And mess up my good thing? Hell no!" She frowned at him. "They seen it on you, man. They got sharper sight than me. They read you plain the second you pass the door. Took me gettin' close to see it."

"Then what'd they want you to find out from me?"

"Just what you seen. They curious about the Good Gray Man theyselves. Don't nobody know nothin' 'bout him for sure. 'Cept he out there somewhere. But everybody want to learn what they can."

"You buy all this crap?"

" 'Bout the Good Gray Man?" She gave a vigorous nod. "Oh, yeah. I be feelin' him from time to time."

Sedele crossed the bar to the woman wielding the mop and spoke to her in harsh tones. The woman bent to her work with renewed energy.

"Arlise!" Nedra called. "I've got to be going!"

Arlise hopped down from the stool. "You want to help Vida, you take her 'way from here. Else she gon' wind up like that poor ol' Madeleine LeCleuse."

"That's bullshit!"

"You don't believe me, jus' hang 'round and watch." She

turned, then glanced back at him. "You the one sent to help Vida. Do what you s'posed to, things'll work out."

"Nobody sent me," he said.

"Big fool, you, for thinkin' that," she said. "Everybody sent by somethin'."

She hurried over to Nedra, who was standing by the door, and followed her out.

Do what you supposed to.

Mustaine knew he should do something, but that was a long walk from knowing what exactly he was supposed to do.

A Springsteen tune blurted from the jukebox, the people's millionaire complaining about the hard times he'd been having, and Sedele, who had punched up the song, stationed herself at the bar three stools down from Mustaine. Her pale features were drawn. She had on a white silk dress sheathed in lace, with a tight, low-cut bodice. It was too young for her. A costume, Mustaine thought; a party outfit.

"Rough night?" he asked.

She stared at her cocktail napkin.

"Me, too," he said with relish. "I hardly slept at all."

"Don't start," she said without lifting her eyes.

Earl set a Cryptoverde on the cocktail napkin. Sedele closed her hand about the glass and told Earl to buy the old man in the seersucker suit a beer. "I don't need attitude from you," she said to Mustaine. "I'm not a happy soul."

"I didn't steal Vida. She came and got me."

"That don't mean I gotta listen to you gloat." Sedele picked up the glass; her pink tongue licked at the crust of foam atop the drink, making a neat half-circuit of the rim. "I won't wish you luck, but I can't wish you ill, neither. Vida gets her life back, maybe it's worth this town goin' to hell."

"Those are the options?"

"So it would appear." She had a sip and her eyelids drooped.

He had an itch to argue, to probe; but then he realized he had all the information he needed on what the people of Grail believed was happening—or going to happen—to Vida.

"I wasn't really gloating," he said.

"I know. You were playing. Like we did last night. But . . ." She took another sip and, affecting a fey Southern-belle delivery, said, "I have put all that behind me."

The unsteadiness of her voice told him that she was half in the bag. He envied her fuzziness of focus. "This town is nuts," he said.

Sedele gave an amused sniff, but did not speak.

"What?" he said.

Her green eyes swung toward him, as if she were picking up a signal and checking him out. She asked Earl for a cigarette. He offered her one from an open pack, lit it for her; she exhaled a thin stream of smoke from between pursed lips and spoke to Mustaine's reflection in the mirror. "I got a thing for weak men with brains. They're intriguing, but not dangerous. So I've decided to like you."

"Gee, thanks."

She held up a hand to hush him. "Reason I trust men like that, they can know somethin', but they not strong enough to believe what their mind's tellin' 'em. Whatever it is they think they know, they truly don't know it, 'cause belief is most of knowledge. So when you say, 'This town is nuts,' what I'm hearin' is, 'This town confuses me.' It's what any weak man with brains would say when he's confronted by a mystery."

"If Grail's a mystery," he said, "so's inbreeding."

Sedele took another hit from her cigarette and blew smoke down into her glass, making the green liquid appear to seethe like a magic potion. "New York, Los Angeles . . . Omaha, you look beneath the surface, it's nuts everywhere. Difference 'tween the rest of the world and Grail, our surface been peeled away for a couple hundred years. We in what'cha might call plain fuckin' view."

The Springsteen song had ended and Chris Isaak's "Wicked Game" began to play.

"Two hundred years," Sedele went on. "Grail's been through depression and disaster, and it's maintained. It hasn't thrived, but it hasn't declined. We been lucky. And the reason we lucky, we cut a deal to guarantee our luck. It might be we cut a deal with the Devil. Nobody knows for sure. But it's done. We hafta live with it." She studied her reflection, patted down her hair. "You better learn to believe in it, too, or you ain't gonna have the strength to do what's necessary."

"And what you figure that is?"

"Don't you know?"

"Oh, yeah. I might take Vida with me when I go. But this thing some of you got like you've known all about it, like I'm walking around with a mystic sign on my brow . . . if that's the case, why hasn't anyone tried to stop me?"

"You think people in this town like what's happenin' with Madeleine and Vida? They don't. They 'fraid of losin' what they got, but they don't admire what they hafta do to keep it. Might be a few put roadblocks in your way, but when it comes down to it, nobody's gonna stop you. Nobody 'cept you . . . and maybe Vida. 'Cause she will *not want* to go with you."

"You don't know that."

"I know Vida better'n you."

"Maybe we just know different things," he said.

Do what's necessary. What you supposed to do.

What if Sedele was right? About everything. What if Grail was merely typical, and the world with its surface peeled away would reveal itself to be a place where shabby magic was intertwined with the laws of physics? The idea of a bargain with the supernatural, a consensus bargain made every single day by billions of prayers and devout accommodations, it would explain a lot of what appeared inexplicable.

Sedele lifted her drink and sang along with Chris Isaak, putting her heart into it.

"Vida." Mustaine said it under his breath.

The sound of the name sent ripples stirring across his deep waters. That a woman he'd known for less than twenty-four hours could affect him so; that she could draw him with such apparent ease into the thicket of her life; that he could drive into town and an hour later fall in love with someone who needed him to be a man and take responsibility: He was tempted to chalk it up to circumstance and adrenaline, but that didn't fit the facts. The most surprising thing, the troubling thing, because he worried he might be conning himself, was that he wanted to do it.

He stared at his glass until the Isaak song was replaced by Dr. John doing "Walk on Guilded Splinters." The eerie chorus of female voices caught on in his head and stalled his thoughts, emptied him, as if he were tweaking on crystal meth. He had a snapshot memory of Vida from the night before, her face in shadow above him, moonlight gleaming on her breasts.

A rag swished across the counter at the edge of his vision, and Earl said, "You nursin' that shot of whiskey like it's the last thing you own. If you low on cash, I'll buy the next one."

Mustaine considered whether he wanted more to drink. He pointed to the rack of Cryptoverde glasses. "Let me have one of those evil things."

Earl beamed and said, "I figgered you'd come around."

13
Twilight Time

$\mathcal{V}$IDA CLOSED THE DINER AT SIX SHARP. WASN'T MUCH
point keeping it open—people started drinking early on
St. John's Eve. She left Anson to lock up and walked briskly
along the shoulder of the road toward Le Bon Chance. Marsh
had backed off her, or else his spells were weakening like he
said. Worn down by her resistance, she told herself. She was
calmer than she had been all day. Her thoughts joined the
hours ahead and the promise of Jack into a mental dance of
anticipation. She pictured herself lying on the bed with her
knees drawn up and him lowering atop her. The image
provoked an immediate physical reaction that, in turn,
caused her step to grow loose in the hips. Oh, she was ready
for this! She'd had to net him, haul him into the boat, too
busy at the task to understand completely how she was feeling, but she could feel it now, yes she could. Half in heaven,
half in heat, all in the arms of Jesus. A flush warmed her
cheeks; a bead of sweat trickled between her breasts, laying a
cool track. She angled across the parking lot, spotted the
pickup rusting at the far end of the building. The next thing

she saw, flaring up and fading like the pop and afterimage of a flashcube, lasting no longer, was her hands on a pair of milky breasts, the face above them sharp in the way of cut glass, gemmy green eyes pulling her in for a kiss. Her feelings tangled with the vision and she had to stop short to untangle them. That bitch Sedele, sometimes she was worse than Marsh. Though her sendings never offered degradation as a pleasure. Vida refused to let that acid shot of Sedele's thoughts steal her joy. She grabbed a deep breath and went forward again.

Jack and Sedele were sitting at the bar, their backs to the door, two stools between them—the kind of distance people keep, Vida thought, when they're acting bristly. That pleased her. She came brightly up, leaned close to Sedele and said, "Hi there, Sedele! I was just thinkin' 'bout you." Then she turned to Jack, blocking Sedele's view and gave him a soft kiss. "How you doin', baby? You not too drunk, are you?"

"What you got in mind?" His arm went around her waist and gathered her in.

"I can't tell you. I gotta show you."

Getting to his feet, he pretended to be weary. "Oh . . . okay." He dropped a twenty onto the bar and put his arm around her. "See ya," he said to Sedele who was watching herself, frozen-faced, in the mirror.

Vida waggled her fingers in a wave as Jack drew her away. "'Bye now!"

"Mmm-hmm," Sedele said distractedly, her eyes never straying from the puzzle of her reflection. "Catch ya later."

Jack drove. Vida rested her elbow out the window and let the warm Gulf wind close her eyes and saltify her skin. The sky was clearing out over the water, washing to pale blue. They still had better than two hours until dark. "Feel like a swim?" she asked, and pointed up the road. "Pull on past the cabin . . . where the brush starts. I'll show you my pond."

She took a rolled-up blanket from behind the seat and led Jack through the bushes and the bamboo. Once they reached the pond she shucked off her dress and panties. She dived straight into that dark bedeviled water, swimming nearly a length beneath the surface, shooting up into the air in time to see Jack dive. He came up spouting. Caught her waist and dragged her under in a slippery embrace. His hands molded her into a new figure of desire, squeezing her waist narrow, reshaping her breasts to fit the hollows of his palms. They played that way a while, then clambered onto the bank, fell onto the spread blanket and made love. It was so sweet and normal, so devoid of strangeness, Vida was made paranoid. Afraid it wasn't real, then afraid it was. So accustomed was she to the imposition of the perverse, deliverance from it seemed abnormal. But soon she gave herself over to the union of Forms and the magic of a single flesh. Jack moaned and the same song went sighing out from her. Knowing what he knew, she moved to turn onto her side an instant before he signaled her to. Feeling what he felt, as he thrust feverishly into her, her own urgency spiked, spilled all through her and floated her soul off on an explosive tide as her hips convulsed. A white darkness concealed her from herself and she came. It was like, she thought afterward, they had vanished into one another, beamed into each other's bodies like on *Star Trek*. She drifted in and out for a time. Her vision blurred, transforming leaves and patches of sky overhead into a dome tiled with a mosaic of dark green and lavender gray. The concatenation of silence that had engulfed her gradually was eroded by rustles, chirps, gurgles. She could not recall if she had blurted out that she loved him. She wanted to tell him that very second; she knew it was right. But she was so tired. Heat faded from her skin and she slept.

Mustaine watched her sleep until her eyelids began to flutter. "What you doing?" he asked, and that woke her completely.

The sky was going purple and stars were out, burning holes in the canopy; the moon was hidden somewhere off behind the thickets, but she felt its presence. She rubbed her eyes. He was half a shadow sitting beside her. His knees drawn

up. Wearing a T-shirt and briefs. Giving her a serious look. The Form almost fully seated inside him.

"Hey, sweetie," she said, sitting up and stretching.

His eyes fell to her breasts, to the pouches of muscle supporting their weight. "Christ," he said. "You are so beautiful."

She leaned back and braced herself on both hands, liking the feel of his regard. "I ain't been around anyone uses that word for a while. They say things like, 'You got great tits, Vida,' and 'Man, you must got a motor in your ass.' But 'beautiful' wasn't in their vocabulary. Know what I think? I don't think I was beautiful for them. I don't think I been beautiful for a long time."

"Moment you came into Le Bon Chance," he said, "all I could see was how beautiful you were."

"Well maybe I *can* be beautiful with you."

He let a silence build, half-listening to the productions of the wind in the leaves. He was wary of saying what he had planned to say, worried that Sedele was right and Vida would not leave Grail. But he couldn't *not* say it. "I realize it's quick . . . it's only been a day. But I want you to come with me to Florida."

A Christmas star of relief and happiness lit up inside Vida's head, dominating the lesser constellations of her thoughts. The Form had made itself known. The man, too. They were a unity and now change was possible. She was so happy, she wanted to tease him. "And leave my business?" she said. "Just like that, I'm supposed to give up everything I worked for?"

Taken aback by her vehemence, he couldn't come up with a response.

"Leave the glorious life provided me by the diner?" she went on. "The delightful company. The pleasant hours. All so I can go live in a beach house with the man I love? How can you ask it of me?"

He felt something in himself expand at the words "the man I love," as if a faulty connection had been suddenly cleared up. "I love you," he said, and reached out to caress her cheek.

She settled back on the blanket and looked up at him. The moon peeked over the top of the thickets, brightening brights, darkening darks. The shadows of his eyes had deepened, like irregular cuts in a mask, and maybe shadow was a conductor of thought, because she gained a sense of her body from what seemed a shared perspective, both as a topography of moon-pale flesh and a map of sensations: the hardness of the earth beneath her; a pulse in her neck registering the passage of life; the soft clutter of breath in her throat. She knew her scent was rising to him from the wetness between her legs, and she wanted him to touch her there. Closed her eyes and willed him to touch her. Anticipation made her all nerve and notice. His fingers grazed her curly hair and when they pressed against her, opening her, jolts of feeling went splintering into her belly and melted warm all through her. She thought if she could hear the sound of her pleasure, it would be a delicate crackling like that of a small fire. She let her knees fall apart and encouraged him to come atop her.

"I'll go with you," she said.

They made love beneath a latticework of leaves and stars, while the moon climbed and Thalia's Pond was transformed from a shaded oval into a glittering black pupilless demon eye of water staring up at the canopy that imprisoned it, unmindful of the mutant creature being born on its banks amid groans and soft cries, obeying the rule of the oldest rhythm. Braced above her, with his head down, Mustaine imagined briefly that he was a shadow cast by a radiant, turbulent force beneath, and Vida had an instant of self-awareness during which she saw the lumpy yellow moon caught in the crotch of a forked, leafless branch, like a magic stone in the thong of a slingshot, aimed directly at her, a sight that Marsh persuaded her to see; then the thong was loosed and the stone flew at her, an uncommonly slow flight that gave her a second to be afraid before it struck, showering her with a splash of harmless golden light. The rest was thoughtless, or else thought itself had turned as sharp and inarticulate as feeling.

They were all feeling for the longest time. Words passed between them, but these were mere symptoms, valueless noise. Then Vida's soul flicked inside her, a tongue of heat upon whose tip her sexy particulars were balanced like a crystal saliva pearl, and she sang out a Name she'd spoken no more than once or twice before, just vowels and a broken melody, and a heartbeat later Mustaine went shuddering out of himself, spilled his entire substance forth, and fell half-atop her, dazed as a husband spider the moment before his lover consumes his legs. And there they lay, gasping, beaded with sweat, blessed by a secret knowledge they were already beginning to forget.

The wind shook itself like a wet dog in the crown of a water oak and began to lash up the thickets, getting the stalks of bamboo to bend and clack against one other. Ripples like miniature sets of ocean waves piled across the surface of the pond. Mustaine and Vida dressed slowly and walked back to the truck. He took the keys from her and kicked over the engine, pumping the gas to make it run smooth, and as he sat there, letting it idle, Vida leaning against him, one arm about his shoulders, he felt a pull inside him as if the freshets of wind had kicked him over, started up his engine.

"I think we oughta go now," he said. "Just grab what you need from the cabin and we'll get outa here."

"What 'bout your car?" she asked, easing back from him so she could have a better look at his face.

"I'll get you situated down in New Smyrna, then I'll come back for the rest of your stuff and the car."

"There's things I gotta do. I can't just up and leave. Tomorrow's soon enough."

He felt the pull again, like a tide this time, bearing his soul forward and half out of the body. "Come on, Vida. Do it for me."

"I can't! Even if there wasn't no other reason, it's Saint John's Eve. I hafta be here to pass the scepter."

"Fuck the scepter! We can be in New Smyrna before tomorrow night."

His insistence vexed her—she didn't know why he was

being so unreasonable. "I hafta be here," she said firmly. "Just take it easy, all right? We gonna have fun tonight. Saint John's Eve's 'bout as much fun as Grail ever gets. I'm tellin' you, you don't wanna miss it."

Troubled but not understanding why, Mustaine put the truck in gear and drove toward the cabin. Then drove on past it.

"What you doin'?" Vida grabbed for the wheel, but he held her off. She made another, more forceful try, but he was too strong for her.

"I want you to stop!" she said. "Right this second!"

The left front tire dipped into a pothole and she had to catch hold of the dash to keep herself from being thrown into Jack.

"Goddamn it!" She opened her door a crack. "You don't stop, I'm gonna jump! I swear I will!"

Reluctantly, he slowed the truck, shifted into park.

"What is wrong with you?" She punched his arm hard. "You gone crazy?"

"I got a feeling we should go now," he said.

"Good Lord! I listened to every feelin' I got, I'd be twisted in knots like a pretzel."

"It's really strong. I . . ."

She couldn't tell if she was seeing the man or the Form, they were so purely blended now, and that sparked her to think maybe she should heed what he was telling her, maybe it was the Form talking. Then again, maybe it was the man, fallible and desiring. She'd thought that once love had been secured, she would be able to distinguish between them. But what if she hadn't secured love, what if saying "the man I love" hadn't been a sufficient declaration to set the spell? Surely she must have spoken the words when they were lying by the pond. They had been in her to speak. She couldn't remember. Panicked, suddenly uncertain of herself, of Jack, of everything, she said, "I love you." But the second she said this, she realized that if she hadn't said them before, saying them tactically now, saying them without the weight of her whole feeling, would only weaken the connection.

"I love you," he said, bewildered by her panicked expression and by her strangely freighted delivery of the endearment.

"Look here!" She waved her hands as if to clear away a mist from between them. "I'm goin' with you, okay? You don't hafta worry. But I got my duty to perform. We can leave soon as I've done. The very second! I promise! All right?"

"Yeah, okay," he said. "But I . . ."

"But nothin'!" She collapsed against him, all softness and warm honey, and kissed him. "You ain't goin' nowhere without me, you understand? You gonna hafta scrape me off with a trowel, you try and get rid of me."

The wind stopped blowing abruptly, as if it had flat quit on whatever it was hoping to do—the pull inside of Mustaine stopped with the same abruptness. He felt undelivered, as if deliverance had been near to hand.

"My goodness, me," said Vida, chucking him under the chin. "Look at that mournful face you wearin'! Like all the ghosts just rung their bells for you. You pick yourself up, lover, y'hear? Put on that rock 'n' roll attitude. We goin' to a party."

14

St. John's Eve

*J*UST THE TOWN SIDE OF THE DIRT ROAD THAT HAD brought Mustaine to Madeleine LeCleuse's cabin in the swamp lay the winding asphalt road that led to the housing development where the solid citizens of Grail lived, and farther along, to Joe Dill's acreage on the Gulf. The Midsummer Queen's coronation was always held, Vida told him, at the home of the luckiest person in Grail, and since he was the richest, Joe Dill had been deemed to be that person. Vida didn't agree with this standard of measure, but she had to admit that Joe Dill threw a hell of a party. She told Mustaine about St. John's Eves past as they drove. She had on heels and a slinky green silk dress with spaghetti straps and a plunging neckline and a sheath skirt slit up to the thigh. If he had only just met her, he thought, his eyes would have bugged out like a cartoon lecher's—he wasn't altogether certain they weren't bugging out now. He had on a thin black-leather sport coat, jeans, and a white dress shirt. His cheeks shadowed by a day's growth of beard. Vida thought he looked splendid, the Form come full into his body, the man assuming the Form.

Past the development was a stretch of cleared grassy land, half-drowned in a pointillist mist, and upon it had been constructed several blocks of a city street lined with white-washed buildings, most two and three stories tall, many sporting neon signs. Some of the signs spelled out English names; others used Vietnamese characters. Leaning wooden poles supported telephone and electric lines. Washes of red, purple, and yellow light sprayed from doorways and windows, staining portions of the mist, causing the scene to have the pale coloration of an antique hand-painted postcard. At the end of the street was a small French colonial church of yellowish stone with a high steeple where, Vida said, Joe Dill lived with Tuyet.

Mustaine found a slot for the truck among the hundreds of vehicles parked on the grass, then he and Vida walked hand-in-hand onto the street, joining the crowd that circulated along it. The ambience was '60s Saigon and the buildings housed brothels, hotels, titty bars, herbal shops, restaurants, and so on. Salted in among the citizens of Grail were Vietnamese hookers in halter tops and hot pants; young unsmiling Vietnamese men sitting astride motor scooters, dressed in silk shirts and jeans, like the old Tu Do Street cowboys; GIs in neatly pressed R&R khakis; old women sitting curbside selling fruits and vegetables out of shallow straw baskets. From inside the Miami Show Bar came live music, a rock band doing a ragged version of "Fortunate Son." The smells were of spices and incense, gasoline and fish sauce. Mustaine recalled Joe Dill saying something about his place, some reference to its Vietnamese atmosphere, but he would never have suspected such a letter-perfect conceit. The press and urgency of the street, its desperate party mode, made him uneasy, as he imagined its original must have affected anyone new to it; and seeing people he had met in Grail taking their ease—Nedra and Arlise, the cop who had hassled him, and others—boosted his anxiety. He understood more clearly than ever that he did not know where he was. He had not known ever since his arrival, but now the recognition was sharp in him, and he wished he had been more forceful in his determination to leave with Vida.

Laughing, saying "Hi" to everyone, possessed of uncustomary good spirits, Vida dragged him into the Miami Show Bar. They entered just as the band kicked into an off-key rendition of "A Whiter Shade of Pale." Fronting the band, on a low stage washed by sweeps of purple, red, and green spotlights, five of the hookers were dancing languidly. Clad in thongs; their small high breasts barely jiggling; bored-looking. Mustaine was right with the music, feeling kind of seasick, and the crowd, roaring, drinking, groping one another at dimly lit tables, called out for more and reached with grasping fingers toward the indolent dancers. Coils of smoke drifted above their heads. Some people began applauding and Mustaine saw that they were staring at Vida, beaming, happy to see her, a reaction contrary to their brooding contemplation of her at Le Bon Chance. Even Sedele was happy. She sprang at Vida from a shadowy corner, drew her into a brief embrace and shouted over the music, "I'm so glad you're here!" Then she kissed her cheek and returned to her private darkness. An enormously fat man in slacks and a dress shirt beckoned to Vida, inviting them to join him and his friends at their table. Vida tried to pull Mustaine toward the table, but he told her to go ahead on, he was going to get a drink at the bar. He stationed himself to the side of some fake GIs—at least he assumed they were fake—and ordered a beer from the Vietnamese bartender, a wiry, disaffected man wearing a short-sleeved shirt over his slacks. He drank slowly, trying to settle his thoughts, half-listening to the guitar player wrecking Robin Trower's solo.

The band went on break, their caterwauling replaced by dance music turned low, and a woman's voice spoke at his elbow, saying, "Hey, GI! You got American cigarette?"

It was Tuyet, dressed as a hooker.

"I don't smoke," he said. "Where's your boyfriend?"

"Me no got boyfriend." She pouted and laid a hand on his arm. "You Number One, GI. Me love you long time."

"Fuck off." He sipped his beer, glanced at the dancers who were frugging to Sly and the Family Stone.

Tuyet bummed a cigarette from the bartender, took a light from him as well, and breathed smoke at Mustaine. "You're in the wrong war, civilian."

"I don't need your act, okay."

"What you need isn't a matter of concern to me."

"Yeah, I got that."

"No, you don't. You don't get any of it." She blew a smoke ring, then poked the cigarette through the middle of it and smiled at her own cleverness.

"Fuck you do around here?" he asked. "You just part of the atmosphere . . . is that it?"

"I consult," Tuyet said.

"You consult. Right. Like when ol' Joe gets a wart on his dick, you tell him, 'It's okay, honey.' "

"That, too." She tired of the cigarette, dropped it and ground it out under a spike heel. "I read his tea leaves."

"Joe doesn't look much like a tea drinker."

"He's discovered its virtues. If you know how to read them, the leaves show you what's coming." She waggled her fingers in his face like a witch working a spell. "I saw you coming, loverboy."

She held his eyes for a three-count and her laugh accumulated, a giggle evolving into a descending musical passage, lapsing into an amused sigh.

"I came to give you your car keys." She dipped two fingers into the cleavage of her halter, extracted the keys, and dropped them into his hand. They were warm from contact with her skin, though not so warm as he might have expected.

"I thought it wouldn't be fixed 'til tomorrow."

"Joe had them rush the job. It's parked at Le Bon Chance."

"Tell him 'thanks.' "

"Tell him yourself. You'll see him at the coronation." She arched her back and her breasts swelled from the halter.

"Not if I can help it. I've had enough of this shithole."

"But you *can't* help it," she said. "If you don't know that, you don't know anything." She turned, and with a toss of her hair, she glanced at him over her shoulder. "Go home, GI. Go back to your own country."

She sauntered off toward the rear of the club and Mustaine had some more of his beer, now tepid and bitter. He watched Vida do a shot at the table with the fat man and his friends. She appeared to be having fun. He caught a glimpse of Arlise staring at him. She shook her head ruefully and looked away. He nursed the beer for fifteen or twenty minutes, then ordered a shot of whiskey. Handed the bartender a ten-dollar bill. The bartender waved it away and said, "Joe Dill say you drink free, GI."

"What's with the pidgin English, man? Is it a gig or what?"

"Actually," said the bartender, "I find it demeaning, but the man pays well."

"You live in Grail?"

The bartender shook his head. "I own a club over in Panama City. Dill brings my whole staff in to run the Miami for this one weekend. The guy's a psycho, but like I said, he pays for what he wants."

"A psycho? How so?"

The bartender's expansive gesture seemed to reference the entirety of the street. "This doesn't say it for you?"

"Hey, man!" It was the kid whose guitar he had borrowed. Cody. "Wanna sit in with us?"

Mustaine hadn't realized Cody was part of the band—he understood the wrecked Robin Trower solo now. "I don't know your tunes."

"Play whatever you want. Play what you did last night. We'll back you up."

A minute later Mustaine was strapping on Cody's Tele-caster; after another minute he was on stage playing. He didn't feel the music as he had the night before. The falsity of the club restrained him, and yet at the same time he had the impression that the Miami Show Bar was almost real, almost Saigon. The spirit of that sad and bloody milieu successfully invoked. The topless bar girls painted lavender and rose by the spots, writhing like colored ghosts in the smoky air, and

Something was bothering Jack again, his mouth was all tight and unsmiling. Vida caught his chin in her bunched fingers and shook him gently. "I wish you'd relax! Won't be long 'fore we outa here and headin' east. We can drive a couple hours, then get us a motel."

"I was thinking we'd drive straight through," he said.

"No . . . un-unh. Nosir! We don't wanna do that. What you need to do is drive us to Biloxi and find us a room at the nicest motel in town."

He was smiling now. "That's how you see things going, huh? Things'll work out best we do it your way?"

"Oh, yeah," she said. "I promise!"

Mustaine couldn't recall whether he'd had any expectation of the coronation, other than that it would be cheesy, stupid, a drag. He could not have predicted it would have any effect on him except, perhaps, to increase his impatience to be gone. But from the outset he felt an occult menace, an impression he tried unsuccessfully to rationalize in terms of his having overdosed on the weirdness of Grail. More than a thousand people lined the misted street, talking murmurously, like a crowd awaiting the opening of theater doors. No music could be heard. Acting the part of an army officer, dressed in fatigues—jacket, cap, pants—Joe Dill paced about at the center of the street, occasionally speaking into a walkie-talkie and receiving static-garbled replies. A good many of his Vietnamese bit-actors had removed themselves from the scene and were leaning out upstairs windows. Vida was standing in front of the yellow church, holding a club of twisted dark wood as if it were a bouquet, looking relatively self-possessed, and Mustaine had secured a position thirty feet down from her, in among people he hadn't previously met, though several of them smiled and said hello. Their simple village friendliness, so untypical of the town, heightened his anxiety. Then Joe Dill waved his arm, retreated back into the crowd, and all the talking stopped. Everything was muffled. Heartbeat-quiet. Just stirrings. The mist thinned and thickened

the tables of buzzcut khaki-clad drunken GIs, and the Tu Do cowboy-types standing around in small groups, arms folded, stern, too cool for this rowdy, stupid, American heat. The illusion started to act upon Mustaine. Outside were sappers, jungles, and 'villes, not rednecks, swamps, and hick towns. Now and then an explosion, a rocket shrieking overhead. He found a way to integrate these things into the music he had stumbled upon at Le Bon Chance. Employing fewer notes, generating feedback to punch holes in the melody.

The breakdown was more impressionistic this time around, illustrating the mystical sickness of Grail, the brain damage of the night. He felt the guitar was channeling the music from some wiser head, the patterns of notes illuminating the invisible patterns that ruled not only the town, but the world that contained it, the ones that prevented you from realizing dreams, from achieving the smallest transcendence, yet that also protected you from the dangers of transcendence, thereby enforcing a neurotic security, a mediocrity glorious for its stability . . . People were standing and cheering. He supposed it was for the music. Then he saw Vida dancing on stage among the bar girls. Not mimicking their disinterested style. Her dance was all heat and vigor. Like she was working out a violent impulse in 4/4 time. If it had been another night, another woman who had jumped on the stage, he would have played to the moment. He would have moved close and made her twitch faster. But Vida disrupted his focus. Her abandon seemed to have less to do with the music than with derangement, and the crowd's gleeful approval brought home the perversity of their circumstance. He unstrapped the guitar and the rhythm fell apart behind him; the bar girls quit dancing. Vida staggered as if she'd been shot. He crossed the stage, brushing past the bar girls who, with passive-aggressive languor, put themselves in his path, and caught Vida by the waist. She tried to pull away. She blinked, appearing to recognize him, but reacted dazedly. How, he wondered, could she have gotten drunk so fast? Then he realized he had left her alone for almost an hour.

"I want to dance some more," she said, looping her arms about his neck. "Dance with me."

"We can dance outside. Let's go."

As he walked her down off the stage, the band struck up an amateurish version of "Sympathy for the Devil" that, with its lurching, fragmented ineptitude and whined vocals, felt more truly demonic than the original.

"Oh, I love that song!" Vida pushed at his chest, closed her fists and swayed unsteadily, unable to catch the rhythm. "Come on, Jack! Please!"

"Nobody can dance to that shit," said Mustaine, though behind them everybody was dancing.

Drunk, but not so drunk as she had been, Vida sat on the curb with Jack beside her, his arm around her waist. She wished she hadn't done all those shooters with John Guineau and his friends. She hadn't had a drink for years, afraid that drunkenness would lower her defenses against Marsh. But knowing he was gone, she had wanted to celebrate her freedom. She still felt like dancing. Sitting there was like sitting in a comfortably warm flame made of Jack and tequila, but she wanted to move, to liberate herself from the vestiges of woe. The Form had done its promised work. She was one answered prayer closer to the mainline of life, and once she got away from Grail, once she settled on the shores of a different ocean, New Smyrna, and God! What would that be like. . . ? Once she got away from Grail, even if Marsh regained his strength, she would be beyond him.

She bumped Jack with her shoulder, trying to rouse a smile. He just sat there like a crooked black stick turned into a man, brooding over something . . . she didn't care what. She'd put a smile on his face before the night was through. She looked off along the street. The mist had thickened; it was getting downright hard to see and almost everybody was inside one or another of the bars. The only people in sight were a handful of Joe Dill's Vietnamese. Some boys with motor scooters, old women, a slim coppery-colored man in shorts sitting cross-legged across the way, repairing a bicycle

that was propped upside down in front of him. Vida liked it better where she was crowned Queen. Out on Beauford Monroe's estate. Sedele's daddy. That night had been misty same as this. Beauford had set metal torches everywhere outside and they had gleamed like foxfire in the misty dark. Here, with all these bright electric lights, it wouldn't half be so pretty.

"How long's it all going to take," Jack asked. "This coronation deal."

"Half-hour, maybe. Little more." She caressed his hair. "Don't act so put upon! You might enjoy it."

"I doubt it."

"You might! For me, most of the fun is tryin' to guess how they choose the queen."

"Don't they just vote . . . or have judges?"

"Oh, no! See it's gotta be like the Good Gray Man does the choosin'. So they let him speak through somethin' of nature."

He flashed her a quizzical look.

"My year, they did the choosin' with a serpent. They dragged a big ol' blacksnake outa the swamp, and whichever of us it wriggled up to, she'd be the queen."

"I woulda wriggled up to you . . . it'd been me."

"You ain't no snake." She leaned her head back into his shoulder. " 'Cept sometimes."

The mist was growing thicker, stained into zones of hazy color by the neon and the lights from inside the bars, and Vida thought maybe it would be a pretty coronation after all, the little girls in their white dresses walking through gauzy scarves of lavender and green and rose.

" 'Course there was some controversy when I was chosen," she said. "I musta stepped on somethin', some dead critter, and got blood on my shoe. So when the snake come to me, some said it was 'cause it smelled the blood on my shoe and they accused my mama of puttin' it there. Which was a lie. There was dogs everywhere 'round the place where I was chosen. They're always killin' squirrels . . . cats. Probably I stepped in some ol' piece of a barn cat."

with an oddly vital irregularity, as if it were being circulated by process of some failing organ.

Something was approaching from the east end of the street, resolving from a white disturbance inside the mist into three pretty little girls in lacy white communion dresses: two brunettes flanking a redhead. Bearing sheaves of what appeared to be flowering weeds. They walked abreast of one another at a slow, obviously practiced pace, their eyes straight ahead, expressions sober . . . though Mustaine thought the redhead was repressing a smile. When they reached Vida they turned as one and stood beside her, facing back the way they had come. Vida shifted her feet, adjusted her grip on the club. She gazed in his direction. He waved, but she didn't seem to notice the gesture.

The silence of the crowd was oppressive, beating in against Mustaine. His chest tightened and he felt a pulse in his neck. He peered off along the street. Something big and dark materialized from the mist. Mist congealed around it, nearly hiding it from view, then dissipated enough for him to see an enormous longhorn steer with a dark red coat and a white patch on its face. The boy leading it was about fourteen or fifteen, and the top of his head was lower than the beast's shoulder. The tip of its horns were at least seven feet off the ground. It shook its massive head and expelled a bellows sound as it passed. Mustaine was amazed that the girls, confronted with this barnyard freak, could maintain their poise, but they seemed unconcerned. Vida, however, had become agitated.

Close behind the steer followed a gray figure that, after a moment of alarm, Mustaine recognized to be a man covered from head to foot in gray cloth, effecting a Gumby look. Holes for eyes, but otherwise featureless. He would scoot toward the crowd with a rolling gait, flapping his arms as if they were boneless; then freeze in place and stand without moving. Mustaine thought of the gray figure he had seen in the swamp and wondered if the performance was based on observation.

The steer stopped a couple of feet away from the girls. Again as one, they stretched out their hands, offering it their sheaves of weeds. The boy let the lead rope fall, and the steer tossed its head. It was a disturbing sight, this monstrous hot creature with heaving sides looming over the delicate little girls in their lace finery. Mustaine had a vision of the steer lowering its head, hooking with its horns, and white blood-stained dresses, tiny disemboweled bodies tumbling through the air. But it only edged forward and sniffed at the weeds. Somebody behind Mustaine gasped, apparently believing that the steer had chosen the brown-haired girl on the right; but the animal proved to be picky and sniffed each bunch of weeds in turn, before taking a cautious bite from the other brunette's bunch. The gray-clad man leaped high; cheers burst from the crowd as they poured into the street. Mustaine lost sight of the girls, of Vida—he never saw her pass the scepter. He pushed toward the steer, whose horns showed above the heads of the crowd, but by the time he reached the spot he had headed for, the steer apparently had been led away. He saw the redheaded girl. She looked sad. A redheaded woman in jeans and a plaid shirt was offering consolation.

Not a sign of Vida, though.

The street cleared, the crowd flowing back into the bars from which music once again began to issue. Stragglers stood about in small groups. Mustaine thought Vida had likely returned to the Miami, but he worried that she had not. The coronation, despite its grotesque imagery, had not been overly disturbing; yet he had a feeling he had missed something. That something had occurred outside his field of vision and Vida was involved. He walked toward the parked cars, thinking he would make a circuit of the street before heading for the Miami. Not seeing her, he became frantic. He started off one way, walked a few paces, then changed his mind and headed in the opposite direction. As he passed some men talking, Joe Dill broke off from the group and fell into step beside him.

"You not leavin', are ya, man?" he asked. "Party's just gettin' started."

"I'm looking for Vida. You seen her?"

"She's off somewhere, don't you worry."

The forced casualness of his tone set off Mustaine's detectors. He confronted Joe Dill. "You know where she is?"

"Couldn't say."

"Tell me where the fuck she is!"

"Off doin' her civic duty," said Joe Dill. "Givin' her all for good ol' Grail." He removed his cap and got into Mustaine's face. "You been a pain in the ass since the second you got here, man. Y'know? Sneerin' at us . . . lookin' down your nose. You don't know shit about us. This town takes care of its own. We face up to what we do." He jabbed two fingers into Mustaine's chest. "Whatever your part was in all this, it's done. You got no place here now. Time for you to be movin' on."

"Where the hell is she?" Mustaine insisted.

Joe Dill gave his fatigues a pat-down. "Guess she musta fallen outa my pocket." He grinned. "I gotta coupla spare hookers at the Miami, you lookin' to upgrade."

A surge of anger overrode Mustaine's natural caution. He pushed Joe Dill, sent him reeling back, but not down.

"Whoo-ee!" Having regained his balance, Joe Dill put hands on hips and regarded Mustaine with mock admiration. "You a regular killin' machine! The ol' two-handed shove . . . Don't believe I ever seen it used with such deadly efficiency."

"Tell me what the fuck is going on! Where is she?"

"I *should* tell you, y'know? I should send you after her and let your sorry ass get all fucked up."

The way he said this, the words, the tone: they confirmed Mustaine's suspicion that something bad was happening to Vida. Yet the notion that this entire magical mystery tour of Good Gray Men, witch men, Midsummer Queens, and a town of clairvoyants had the slightest reality . . . even in the moment he believed it, he didn't completely believe it. But he cast disbelief aside and went at Joe Dill again, taking him by surprise, knocking him flat with an amateurish, looping, yet mystically directed right hand. He kicked him in the stomach, the legs. He cursed him, kicked him in the hip. Then he stumbled back, breathing hard. The group of men who had been talking with Joe Dill were watching, but showed no inclination of coming to his aid.

"Where is she?" Mustaine toe-rolled him onto his back.

Blood trickled from the bridge of Joe Dill's nose onto his lips, painting a red line down the center of his face. His left eyelid was cut and swollen. Nonetheless, he wheezed out a laugh. "You want it that bad, I won't stand in your way." He heaved up onto an elbow. "You do a lot better takin' your little car and your faggoty guitars and gettin' yourself on down the road. But since you asked . . ." He spat a glob of pink saliva, wiped his mouth on his sleeve. "Back of the church there's a trail runs off into the swamp. She'll be on that trail right 'bout now."

Mustaine hesitated and Joe Dill chuckled. "Didn't Vida set her spell on you? She set it on me, that's for sure. I'da gone through fire for that woman back in the day. She must not have got you good as she got me. 'Least you don't act like she did."

Suspended between disbelief and belief, fear for himself and fear for Vida, Mustaine set out walking toward the church, slowly at first, then with purpose.

"Ain't you gonna run? Ain't she worth runnin' after?"

Mustaine kicked it into a jog.

"That ain't gonna get it done!" Joe Dill shouted. "Oh, man! You never gonna catch up to her! Not movin' that slow!"

Desperation and shame caught up with Mustaine and began wrestling for his soul. He broke into a sprint, arms pumping, the yellow church jolting sideways with every step. Some of the young guys sitting astride their motor scooters were jeering and urging him on, and a few people had emerged from the bars and were staring with consternation. As if worried about what he might do. That spurred him faster.

"There you go, man!" Joe Dill's voice was fading. "That's more like it! Now you gotta chance!"

Feeling disconsolate and not understanding why, Vida took herself off back of the church after passing the scepter to Jeannette Lamoreaux, needing a moment alone to pull her thoughts together. Maybe, she thought, being the Midsummer Queen had meant more to her than she had known, because now she was queen no longer, she felt a lack inside her. Her fears of the future went to tumbling around inside her head like a load of dirty laundry on the rinse cycle.

The mist was thicker here, seeming to glow whitely, wrapping the cypress trees beyond in luminous ribbons like the ghosts of rivers wending their way into the nothing they sprang from. Vida stood on the edge of the lawn that extended from the church, at the foot of a path that led off into the cypress, and wished she'd gone when Jack wanted. Then she would still be Midsummer Queen in her own mind, she would never have relinquished the one thing that had made her feel special.

That wasn't true, she told herself. Jack and the Form, they made her feel special too.

"Hey, Vida!"

She wheeled about, saw a gray figure walking out from the mist alongside of the church, and before she recognized it for Jeannette's daddy, Pinky Lamoreaux, in that dumb gray costume of his, she let out a squawk and threw up her hands to ward him off.

"Jesus Christ, Pinky!" Her right hand went to her heart, which was thumping wildly. "Whyn't you take that stupid thing off?"

"It's too damn hot's why. I ain't wearin' nothin' underneath," said Pinky, coming up to her. The hood of the costume sucked in toward his mouth when he inhaled. His eyeholes looked empty.

"Well, you give me a fright. What you want?"

"I's hopin' you'd talk to me 'bout Jeannette. 'Bout what it's gonna be like for her . . . being queen and all."

She studied on the question, parsed out its meaning. "She ain't gonna be like me, that's what you worryin' 'bout. Jeannette's a real sweetheart. She don't have the wildness in her I had. I always had it in me. Wasn't bein' queen made it come."

"That ain't what I'm askin'." Pinky held out his gray paws as if in supplication. "What I'm wonderin' on is how you feelin' now."

"I feel fine. I'm a little sad. I mean—"

A figure materialized from the mist behind Pinky. Much larger than him. Darker gray, like trash-fire smoke grown solid. It put its fingerless hands on Pinky, lifted him up, and he went to trembling all over and making muffled explosive sounds, as if trying to suppress a bad cough. Blood plastered the face of his mask to his mouth and chin, lending them shape. Then he was sailed up and out into the swamp. There came a sodden splash. The figure loomed over Vida. Its particulars overwhelmed her. Not like smoke, she thought. Like a smudge, a stain whose outlines shifted, its edges fraying, shrinking, and expanding. Though it had no eyes, she could feel its eyes branding their oval shapes onto her brain, and though it had no fingers, she felt fingers grip her waist hard like cypress forks, drawing her in, submerging her in its gray substance, which was electric and terrible, a gray fire tingling all through her . . . *He* was all through her, she realized, and that knowledge kindled her fear in a strike that sent every other thought scattering and lit a scream in her throat that must have brought blood with it, it was so desperate, so final and despairing. Then, as if the sum of her fear had been used up in that awful flaring scream, she was diminished, pared down to a primitive awareness capable only of knowing one thing, but of that one thing knowing almost everything.

She knew him, knew his nature.

He had been a man, but now was trapped in the in-between, the emptiness between times and universes and conditions, the ultimate nowhere, and he was trying to make a place for himself, to haul himself back into the here-and-now from the not-there-and-never. Because he was not quite here or anywhere, he had become more than simply a man who once had been—he was now all those almost-things that aligned with his nonbeing, that had conspired with his thoughts to transform and destroy him while he lived. The desolate ghost of lost love. Desire reduced to madness. Yearning honed to violent need. Regret fractioned into a bitter keening trouble along the nerves. She saw as through his eyes a patch of clarity, the shape of a locket picture opened in the gray surround, an Acadian woman with chestnut hair. Not a virgin—far from it—yet virginal to his touch. Vida knew he was trying to match her up with the woman. Not their looks—though they might have been reflections of one another—but their hearts.

Was she, like that woman, still open to love?

For an instant she believed she was. And he believed it—he recognized her. She experienced his shock at the recognition, his dawning happiness. But then he became confused and she felt the cold burn of his displeasure when he found she loved another. The compression of his anger squeezed her thin and juiceless, until she was a pale thread woven through his shadow heart. She began to lose consciousness, to go tumbling away from the turmoil of their thoughts, mingled like blood and water. But even as she faded, she was given to know his name and from this she understood what had happened. Understood the perverted trick that love and time and maybe some speckled froglike demon of the mist hunched high in a sentry tree overlooking the town had played on them. She tried to tell him none of this was necessary. She loved only him and no other. To prove it she said his name over and over until it had the sound of a grackle cawing in mockery at her fall.

Jack, she said, jack jack jack jack jack jack . . .

She woke standing and in a state of extreme arousal. Naked. Warmth and wetness between her thighs. The place in which

she stood, a filthy cabin with a sagging roof, garbage everywhere, her new green dress crumpled, adding a splotch of
bright color to a nest of mattress stuffing and rags . . . None of
it bothered her. She laughed and touched herself, closed her
eyes when a hot charge shot through her belly. She kept on
touching herself until her knees weakened and she had to lie
down. The grimy bedclothes seemed to crawl up around her
and give her a cuddle.

She closed her eyes again, waiting for him to come, hurry-
ing him with her wish. She'd force him to recognize her
again. Make him acknowledge that he had not been betrayed,
that she was here for him and would give herself utterly,
freely, and without inhibition. He'd realize what had
happened to him, to her, to them, and then this craziness
could stop. When she felt him near she let her knees fall apart
and held out her arms, but kept her eyes closed. She didn't
want to see that gray stain—she wanted the man he had
become, the Form integrated with the flesh, blue-eyed and
deep, not this paring of both that had been splintered off by
the shock of broken love, the product of a wrongly set spell.
He settled atop her, less substantial than a man; but in her
arms he gained solidity, manifesting the lean structures and
prodding heat that she associated with him. When he
plunged inside, a flood of joy and power flowed with him. But
as he began to thrust, he thrust the rest of himself inside. All
the poison of distraction and bitterness. The raw spoilage of
love. He used her violently, blaming her for not being who
she was, not seeing her . . . seeing instead an inadequate
substitute, another Midsummer Queen. Never the right one.
He battered at her, nearly stopping her breath. He had forgotten their moment of mutual recognition, and it was worse
than with Marsh, who—at least—had seen her. Worse even
than the worst of Marsh. His contempt was suffocating her.
Every movement he made, envenomed by contempt, caused
her agony. She felt herself shutting down and understood that
he was using up her light, her force, her soul. He was extract-
ing it like a spider sucking juice from a fly and whatever
remained would be left to sag and mutter and dodder. She

screamed his name, not wanting to die by fractions, to live past death like a roach without a head, wobbling about for no good purpose. To her amazement he answered, calling her name. His voice seemed to issue from a long way off, but it was him. She was certain of it.

"Jack!" she said, locking her legs behind his back, wanting to pleasure him now he remembered . . . though he continued to hurt her. Then, in an eyeblink, he was gone. She drew up her knees, turned onto her side, curling around the pain he'd made. The sour stink of the bedclothes assailed her. She was cold, she didn't know what to do. Life in its profusion, her mama had said, comes to no conclusion but confusion. Everybody said the same thing different ways . . . except for the Jesus shouters, and who knew what they were saying. Hope was out of fashion, but Vida was old-fashioned. She had hope in her now. If he remembered once, he would remember again. She could stand up to a lot so long as she had hope. She didn't have much, just a sprig. But like the aluminum Christmas tree with spray-painted gold leaves her mama kept in the closet, it required no nourishment to survive.

She should pray, she told herself. When in doubt, pray it out. Another of her mama's rhymes. She clasped her hands beneath her chin, tried to concentrate, but no direction offered itself as an avenue along which to beam her message.

Jesus, she thought. How 'bout it, Jesus? You there?

She sang his name, liking the sound of it so much, she strung it into a melody punctuated by preacherlike gasps.

"Jesus . . . uh Jesus . . . uh Jesus . . ."

But the Man from Galilee must have been off banging nails in another quarter.

She tried working the Pan-African side of the street, making up her own prayer tongue the way they did in the Temple of Metabalon.

"*Shaka malava . . . shaka malava hakaan. Okamalau otey osha. Shaka malava hakaan . . .*"

That was better, that got a little something going in the

outer darkness. The god of Gibberish. Long-legged and licorice-skinned. He always made time for Vida. She heard herself uttering chuckling liquid syllables and was pleased by the versatility of her devotions. *Ashamadey kinka kala,* she said to herself, and gave a giggle. She'd pray down any trouble came her way. *Jamiania kucha votaraka shonderay . . .*

Vida's scream was sheared off as Mustaine came out of the brush at the rear of Madeleine's shanty. Rotting away on a point, a broken-down sentry post guarding a reach of black water. The mist had cleared and the moon had swung halfway up the sky, bathing the scene in radiance, making the place appear innocent and rustic. A hideaway under a silvery enchantment. The solemn cypress showing like enormous bones set on end and bleached by ghostlight. He took a step forward, shoving the mountain of his fear ahead of him. He had an urge to call out to Vida, but was afraid something else might hear. He managed finally, to say her name, but it came out a croak. He summoned breath and this time he shouted, "Vidaaaa!"

A frog *kerflopped.*

Mist started to seep out through gaps in the shanty wall.

Each separate tendril eeled forth, lengthening, evolving a connected tendril that itself evolved another tendril, until in a matter of seconds, the swamp was wreathed in white streamers, as if all the mist that had been sucked into the cabin had reestablished the same configuration into which it had been arranged before being needed inside. The silence held a reverberation, a subsonic funeral rhythm.

A wall of mist was forming in front of Mustaine, growing larger and thicker until it blocked both the path and his view of the shanty, swirling in delicate eddies. Hairs prickled on his neck and a sense of *déjà vu* heightened his fear. Nevertheless, he pushed forward. The sense of *déjà vu* intensified; the mist boiled up around him, and he experienced a terrifying slippage. It seemed some vital chemical was leaking out, and as its level dropped, his energy was depleted. He sank to his knees, giddy, head lolling, and fell onto all fours. His breath vomited forth in shuddery grunts. He felt weak . . . on the verge of mortal weakness. As if he were about to puke up his heart. Violent shudders pumped through his gut. He was drowning in symptoms. Fever. Nausea. Double vision. Not doubled images, but different angles on the patch of ground beneath him. Something was sliding out of him . . . but not easily. Stretching a connection part umbilical cord, part soul string, and causing anguish both physical and mental. Some dormant scrap of flesh and self that was suddenly dying to be born, tearing a hole in his flesh, his mind, so it could pour on out. He lost track of his body. A gray shadow filmed his vision. Sweat burned his eyes. And then it was free of him. He was free of it. The connection snapped, the pain receded. His strength gradually returned. He was able to breathe again. To think.

He rolled onto his back and looked up.

Framed by leaden sky and cypress tops, the Good Gray Man was standing over him.

For a long moment Mustaine couldn't move, couldn't blink, transfixed by the sight. Its outline was haloed by mist, fuming at the edges, here expanding, there contracting, as if the mist were both sustaining and constricting it. Its skin, its surface . . . tacky-looking, like undried gray paint, but in flux. The horrid gray paper-sack shape of its featureless head. Half executioner, half monstrosity.

Its arm telescoping, it reached down with a mitten hand, and Mustaine, oddly unafraid, let it touch his shoulder.

The touch made him think of dry ice, so cold it burned. But what he saw, conveyed by the touch (of that he had no doubt), was more painful by far. Vida. Naked, her skin smeared with grime. Her slitted eyes showing crescents of white beneath the lids. Curled up among dirty rags, hands clasped. Muttering nonsense syllables just as Madeleine LeCleuse had done. Mad as rats. The vision faded and Mustaine, seeing that the Good Gray Man was walking toward the shanty, got to his feet. He went a few steps forward and for no good reason, knowing she would not answer, he called out, "Vida!"

The Good Gray Man was suddenly facing him — as if it had reversed itself and not actually turned. It pushed its arms toward Mustaine, hands open, and he was picked up and flung backwards by a hurricane-force gust.

Not of wind, though.

Lying atop a flattened patch of skunk cabbage to the side of the path, trying to regain his breath, Mustaine knew what he had felt. A blast of desolate emotion. Grief and loss and longing welded into a bleak irresistible power.

It was all through him.

Desolation such as he could have never imagined. Yet it was familiar. It suited him somehow, it fit neatly within the fences of his soul. A foul, ingrown self-absorption cooked by years of emptiness into a killing force. And now he felt it was killing him. Tamping down his other qualities, making of his skull a small black space in which to breed its compulsions. He shook his head, trying to knock it loose, but that only seemed to seat it more deeply, to ratify the fact that it had found its rightful place.

He heaved up into a sitting position, one hand braced in the mud. Standing on the bottom step of the shanty, the Good Gray Man lifted his arms in a summoning gesture and the mist that had spread throughout the swamp came at his summons, flowing back to him all in an instant, enclosing him in gauzy white. Then it began to coalesce into a much smaller figure dressed in black coat and a white shirt and faded blue trousers that might have been jeans. Still hazy, rippling. Not quite formed. Its face was pale, difficult to discern. It glanced briefly at Mustaine, as if to warn him off, then mounted the steps and vanished inside.

Dwarfed by the immensity of the swamp, isolate in the silver moonlight, the shanty appeared to have shrunk, become a toy cabin in a kid's mock-up of an evil landscape. Mustaine, still infected by the black emotion that had blown him off the path, confounded by the Good Gray Man's mimicry of his clothing . . . he couldn't get his bearings. He struggled up, gazed about. Every cypress stump and leaf,

every gleaming inch of water, testified to a hopeless knowledge. He had lost her. How it had happened, he wasn't clear.
But that it had was undeniable. He went slogging through the
mud, making an unsteady beeline for the shanty. Intent upon
breaking in, dragging her out. Ignoring the impossibility of
this. But on reaching the rear of the shanty, hearing Vida's
voice issuing from beyond the gapped wall, chanting insane
endearments and garbled prayers, he clamped his hands to
his ears and wobbled away. Pressure built in his chest. He
thought if he opened his mouth, it would come out a howl.

The brightness of the night made him feel exposed, visible
to the silver eye of God, vulnerable to divine strategies. He
imagined he could hear Vida still. Wanting to hide from her
madness, he hurried toward the thickets on the far side of the
shanty, sheltered under the skimpy shadow of a sapling oak. A
path wound off into the thicket—the same path, he remembered, that led to the highway—and seeing it as an answer, a
refuge, an opportunity, he started along it. Turn around, he
thought. But his body knew the truth of things and kept on
walking. He tried to throw out his heart as an anchor, to grab
hold of the branches and spin himself about, to will himself
back to the shanty—but his heart was too light, his fingers too
weak, his mind too filled with despair. For several steps, each
time his foot struck the ground, her name jolted out of him.
Spoken feverishly, viciously, with feral grief. Please God . . .
Jesus, he thought. Send down your holy fucking death ray
and scourge this place. He saw a lake of black glass with burnt
cypress matchsticks poking up from it. He saw a red sun
lowering toward a brackish ocean in which a golden swimmer
drowned. He saw Vida naked on her rags. Vida emerging
from Thalia's Pond, water diamonds spraying from her hair.
Vida sitting next to him beneath the Gulf stars. He saw the
years ahead already shoveled under their graveyard mounds.

Turn around, he told himself.

Soon he began to run.

15

Louisiana Breakdown

*I*T'S A QUIET TIME IN GRAIL, THIS DAY AFTER ST. JOHN'S Eve. All night long folks have been studying cards, tea leaves, shells, the various instruments of divination, and the word is not good. A night upon which the daddy of the new Midsummer Queen is found mutilated on the fringe of the swamp, you wouldn't expect the signs to be real favorable, but then you might not figure they'd be as unfavorable as they are.

Some turn away, pull back before they get a look over the edge. They don't care to see that black bottomland roiling up and belching bubbles. What's known is never equal to what's knowable.

Others deal with the situation.

In the upstairs apartment above Remedies, Nedra Hawes packs her clothes in a steamer trunk that looks to have a hundred drawers, and explains for the tenth time that morning why she can't take Arlise with her to Newport.

"The energies aren't right, dear," she says.

Few minutes earlier, she said the same about staying in Grail.

Arlise is putting on a show of tears, but she's a realist, she realizes Newport ain't her flavor. She's merely trying to negotiate the size of her parting gift.

"Well, I'm gon' come visit you, anyway," she says with lilting menace.

That ruby, pearl, and diamond ring Nedra never wears . . . it's purely Arlise's style.

Most people, though, they just endure. They can't afford to notice the big picture—they got their own fish to fry. They grit their teeth, bow their heads, and let the weather roll across them. Tell 'em the boat they're in is sinking, they'll try to sell you an oar. The signs are everywhere, but they don't care. So the luck of the town has flown . . . so what? They'll keep on keeping on.

Two crabs fighting in the weeds down by the docks, their claws yielding a tiny clatter.

A boy in a Cub Scout uniform standing outside Cutler's Lawn and Garden, waiting for his mom, begins to bleed heavily from the nose.

Off in the swamp, a place where hardly anybody ever goes, a heap of rags nobody will ever find rests facedown in four inches of algae-encrusted water. Straws of gray hair sticking up dry from the soaked scalp. Streams of bubbles issue from the mouths of nibblers beneath the surface.

Adieu, Madeleine . . .

Out on his acreage, his taste of Old Saigon, Joe Dill's looking worse for wear, with his eye stitched and bandaged, curb-sitting in his underpants out front of the Miami, a bottle of Scotch in hand. He tips his head to the weather and spots a seagull falling from the gray, stricken in midflight, dropping out of the big sky movie to become a bug feast.

Leaning in the doorway behind him, Tuyet, wearing a red silk bathrobe, hums a sing-songy tune and smiles as a cat trots past, on its way to investigate the thump.

Yellow rose floating on the surface of Thalia's Pond.

Clifford Marsh used to bring Vida yellow roses, but could be that's a coincidence . . . though he passes through town

now and then. On the sly. Drops in for a drink and a conspir-
atorial chat with Miss Sedele and Joe Dill.

Town business, it's said.

Jeannette Lamoreaux sits on a straight wooden chair
outside her mama's parlor, glumly fingering the lacy dress of
a bridal doll lying on her lap. She misses her daddy, but she's
out of tears for now, worried more about her mama who's on
the sofa sobbing to the preacher. Last time Jeannette peeked
in, the preacher had one arm around her shoulders, which
mama said was an all-right thing to do with boys, and a hand
high on her leg, which mama said was not all right. Jeannette
sees her life changing in a way she cannot express. She knows
the preacher's hand on mama's leg is not a good sign, and she
wishes she had never, ever, ever been chosen the Midsummer Queen.

Housewives' phones are ringing off the hook, people
asking, "Hear what Marjorie saw in the bird's nest this
mornin'?" or "Hear 'bout Larraine's new chart?" or "Hear
what Charlise found in the spider web behind her mirror?"

They've all heard the same thing.

The Good Gray Man's not happy with his woman.

Those among them who can truly see, the hidden seers
and masters of the scene, recognize that it's not that basic.
They see the knot of time and circularity that's been cinched
around the town. Something has happened that no portrait
painted by the cards or graven in lines upon a palm could
ever prophesy. The Good Gray Man and his ribbed original
have come together to be born. There's no denying it. The
signs don't lie. Vida and that no-account guitar player were
both start and finish of the tradition. Why else would the
Good Gray Man have let the boy live, but that he recognized
his own born body and knew he could not regain it? Ain't the
woman he's unhappy with . . . though given the nature of the
Good Gray Man, the paradoxical nature of the event, he
might be unhappy with her, too. But mainly it's the town.
The bargain he made that can't be squared. The thing that
they, the masters, mistook for a spirit proves to be only a

shade, a scrap of wrongly spelled love busted off from the source and slung back two centuries to confuse their ancestors.

A reality loop, a cosmic glitch.

How could this happen? one of them asks.

The laws of physics remain open to interpretation, comes the reply. Magic is singular.

What have we done? questions another.

Lied to ourselves, says another yet. Deluded ourselves.

They begin a doctrinal conversation, debating whether the patterns they perceive in the Tapestry are illusions masking the absence of pattern.

An old lady with an empty shopping bag lapses into self-pity at the liquor store door, finding it closed.

Jadeen Bisette, 15, found comatose in a patch of goldenrod back of Crosson's Hardware. Pronounced dead at 5:44 A.M. Drug overdose. Grail's first ever.

No one has to ask, What's it all coming to?

Cloudy or clear, they get the picture.

Over at Le Bon Chance, bored and gloomy as ever, cynical as a dime bag, Miss Sedele lingers by the jukebox, a pale beringed finger hovering above the buttons. She simply cannot make up her mind between M–257, "Louisiana Breakdown" by Jack Meets Vida, and M–258, "Louisiana Breakdown—Vietnam Mix" by Jack Loves Vida. Finally, for no other reason than her finger gets tired, she jabs at the top button, and the music begins breaking down the moment it was created for, soft grunts and quick-hearted flurries of notes and a slug-nickel tonality, and if you had Sedele's far-seeing eye, you might look down on Le Bon Chance from on high and catch a glint of the music duppy making tracks out the front door, propped open to admit the cleaning staff, and watch the shiny ghost of music flowing along a crack that spreads throughout the world. A shallow crack like a fracture in a veneer caused by something squeezing down on things, closing its fist on the whole shebang. When it shows its palm again, who can say what shapes will remain unbroken.

'Least that's the general feeling in Grail this morning.

While you're up there, gazing down at Le Bon Chance, you might take a gander out along Highway 10 at a little red car what's heading for Florida at an excessive rate of speed, the music duppy hot on its trail, glinting like flecks of mica in the exhaust, desperate to catch up to the one who played it into being. The driver's been crying, going crazy behind something he never had a handle on. Or if he did, he didn't handle it too well. Sometimes his mind's off with Vida on some soft mental surface, making the clumsy low dance of sex and hearing melodies in her hushed breath. Other times he's out behind the shanty in the mist, retreating from a recognition he could not face or comprehend. He doesn't know what happened . . . or maybe he just doesn't want to know. Only thing he knows for sure, though it would not have done any good, he should have tried harder to save her. It was his time to make a warrior move. He can't understand what stopped him. Was it the Good Gray Man or something in himself?

Turn around, he thinks.

But he keeps on driving.

Don't be too hard on the boy. He had magic, fate, human nature, and the Good Gray Man against him.

The wind rips at his face, wildfires his hair. He stares at his eyes in the rearview mirror.

Jammed down out of sight between the back seat and the door, a blue jay feather lashed to a forked twig by a piece of black twine, the wood smeared with brown tarry stuff.

Somebody's going-away present.

Might be a hope charm from a secret friend who never made themselves known . . .

But probably not.

The rain that held off for St. John's Eve is starting to fall. Big cold drops freckling the sidewalks. Storm clouds are contriving a passion of the sky. Hosannas of cloud with silver edges and pudgy faces with pursed lips swelling from their underbellies. Black clouds with lightning spooled in their guts, fat and dumb as gods.

Far out on the Gulf, a waterspout hulas between heaven and earth, its spindly transparent tube twirling in a mockery of grace.

Wind rolls a plastic trashcan along Shinbone Alley.

The WALK sign at the corner of Twelfth and Monroe has gone on the fritz, the brilliant little man made of white dots strobing on and off at fifty apparitions per minute.

People hide behind curtained windows all day, eating comfort food and watching TV, taking a vacation from the truth. Tonight they'll hit the bars early. They'll drink Jaegermeister, green absinthe, and Kalua cocktails, syrupy poisons to purge their spirits, and wind up in the parking lot on hands and knees, strings of bile trailing from their lips. Three sugary twenty-year-old girls with both Sunday school and sodomy on their resumes share a booth and whisper about their hopes and fears, embracing now and then, sharing a cry. Bar fights abound. Sucker-punched bullies with swollen cheeks and split foreheads and chipped molars wince in the fluorescent lights of bathroom mirrors. A rich man tells a whore he loves her and bursts into tears.

Charlie Duhagen, 68, former fireman, kin to the Salt Harvest Duhagens, feeds his pension check into the poker slots and goes home alone.

All penances of a kind.

It's like that everywhere, you say?

No kidding . . .

Mustaine keeps driving through darkest Alabama, then out into the Panhandle of the Sunshine State. He's wind-burned, the skin tight across his face. The frontbone tight across his brain. Thoughts under pressure keen and whistle. He's tempted to let his car drift over the center line, into the high beams. All he wants is Vida. He sees her, tastes her, smells her. He loves her more since he failed her (if failed her he did). That's his penance. It's an act of perfect self-destruction. Songs will jet from his blood. Crescent moons will rise on his fingernails. He has chosen not to rationalize what happened. Not to understand is understanding of a sort. He's aware this is bullshit, but bullshit works for him.

Right now it's working overtime.

He pulls off the highway into a truck stop with a round Sunoco sign atop a pole so high, you can spot it from the overpass. The hard white light of the restaurant sleets like radiation. The paintlike pink make-up on the waitress's cheeks still looks a little tacky. Her lips remind him of those red gelatin lips with syrup inside them he bought when he was a kid.

"Coffee," he says.

TV's tuned to CNN, and the truckers, big-bellied ernies in baseball caps, T-shirts, and jeans, are watching a military medical expert explain the function of a nasal swab—he might be speaking to children, he's talking so slowly, using such simple language. Beneath his image, a red, white, and blue graphic reads AMERICA STRIKES BACK.

Sitting at the counter, Mustaine drops his head into his hands. It's as if he's absent from life, suspended like a shadow among the florid lives of waitresses and truckers and nighthawk tourists. Yet at the same time he's too heavy for the place. Invulnerable as stone. When the waitress says, "Honey, want some eggs or somethin'?" the words set up a resonance in his mind, become a mantra that takes the place of thought, and he has to muster all his concentration in order to shake his head and say, "Unh-uh."

Now he can feel what he never felt before. What he thinks you're supposed to feel, that everybody must feel, the current of life running ragged through him like a handsaw catching on a knot. The effects it produces, love and despair and joy and rage, are only afterimages of its passage. Decaying electron messages, ghosts of a signal. But he and Vida, they were in the moment for a while. They were right there. He holds her name in his mouth like a communion wafer.

Vida.

He thinks about returning to Grail, arming himself in some way against the Good Gray Man. But the hopelessness that afflicted him back in the swamp still dominates his heart.

What, after all, would he find?

Outside the restaurant, the air brakes of an eighteen-wheeler hiss like a twenty-ton vampire. Men are shining flashlights under the trailer, trying to locate a problem.

Way back in the swamp, miles and hours behind, the sound of one woman screaming is heard by no one.

Grail tosses and turns beneath its darkened star.

The Future is fixed. The moving finger has moved elsewhere.

An enormous crumbling sound, like thunder, in the west. The exhausted principle of the first storm. War and rumors of war.

Mustaine's head droops again. He feels terminally weak, devoid of interest or purpose. His battery cracked and leaking acid. The music duppy finally catches up to him, and he seems to hear the closing passages of the song he played in Le Bon Chance, the sweet sting of the metal slide drawing out the last note, letting it hang like a silver tear, and then it falls, plopping into the black despond of history, creating an irrelevant ripple. Then a scraping on the strings; the *bonk* of a metal guitar body against a wooden rest.

Now it's all broken down.

Afterword

*W*AY DOWN AT THE END OF THE MISSISSIPPI RIVER, AT the bottom of the American heartland, where the division between land and sea is not rigorously defined by a single continuous coastline, there really does exist a world not much different from that of Grail. Lucius Shepard knows this world and has lived in it.

For some reason reality gets bent like a heat shimmer coming off the hot asphalt in south Louisiana. Some blame it on rampant alcohol abuse, the roiling tropical heat, or consumption of polluted drinking water. Others claim that our tragic and conflicted past is projecting its skeletal fingers into the present in a karmic act of revenge. Despite a strong Christian presence, the confusing mix of superstitious belief systems, cobbled together from different continents and Caribbean islands, creates something akin to spiritual anarchy. We like to mix things up down here. We throw our left-

overs into the simmering gumbo, combine rural French folk
music with African-American blues, and worship Erzulie
alongside the Virgin Mary. As a man who likes his Christian-
ity straight up, without the voodoo chaser, I must confess I
empathize with Jack Mustaine's flight from romance and the
supernatural manifestations that attend it. Mustaine can't
face up to love, responsibility, or the weirdness he must
confront in Grail, or in himself. So he *doesn't* get the girl and
ride off into the sunset like in so many clichéd Hollywood
films. He fails, bails, and pays for it dearly, but not without
gaining something in the process as "songs . . . jet from his
blood."

I suspect that more than a few readers of *Louisiana Breakdown* will feel Shepard's poetic symbolism resonate in their
bones. Others will experience a strange and hollow feeling in
the pits of their stomachs as they contemplate Vida's dark fate
back at Madeleine's shanty.

This is at it should be, for beneath the splendidly ornate
architecture of this tale lies the spare framework of a human
mythology as old as, or older than, ancient Greek tragedy.
Speaking as an illustrator, I know that Lucius Shepard paints
his canvasses with an unusually broad range of colors when it
comes to subjects of intimacy and tragic love. One can only
acquire such varied hues by using pigments blended from
direct experience. There is no other way.

I have grounded my own illustrations for *Louisiana Breakdown* on the author's vividly described imagery while adding
my own perspective to each creation. Shepard's visual-prose
style gives the artist an overabundance of choice in subject
matter. This is a luxury I rarely have. Invariably there were
many scenes I would have liked to illustrate but didn't. I
avoided some scenes because I felt I couldn't do justice to the
level of the prose, while others remain unrealized because of
publishing restrictions and obscenity laws. In either case I
feel the reader is better left to exercise his or her own visual
imagination.

I first illustrated Lucius's fiction in the pages of *Isaac*

Asimov's Science Fiction Magazine in the early '80s. Our first illustrated hardcover, *The Jaguar Hunter,* was published by Arkham House in 1987 under the editorial direction of the late Jim Turner, founder of Golden Gryphon Press. Jim's brother Gary and his wife Geri currently manage Golden Gryphon along with editor Marty Halpern. Jim has been sorely missed by all of us and we pay special tribute to him with the publication of this book.

I would like to share with you an odd story about the genesis of this volume. Despite the fact that I consider myself a close friend and confidant of Lucius Shepard, I still find him to be an unusually complex and even baffling individual. Lucius actually sent me the first fifteen or twenty pages of this book well over ten years ago. It was a tantalizing excerpt and I expressed my immediate approval and interest in illustrating the story when finished. I remember him describing the basic themes of the remaining story to me in a phone conversation. I was hooked. As fate would have it, though, no other written installments were forthcoming and my mailbox remained empty for all these many years. This was disappointing, but as I have much unfinished work myself I felt I had no right to complain. Other excellent Shepard manuscripts made their way to me in the interim, yet I had to wait until December 2001 to find out exactly how Vida and Jack's story turned out. Coincidentally, I had just returned home to Louisiana after a seven-year stay in New England, so the finished manuscript seemed like an unusually serendipitous welcome-home present. Thank you, Lucius, my friend; you certainly do work in mysterious ways.

J. K. Potter
New Orleans
August 2002

Four thousand copies of this book have been printed by the Maple-Vail Book Manufacturing Group, Binghamton, NY, for Golden Gryphon Press, Urbana, IL. The typeset is Electra, printed on 55# Sebago. The binding cloth is Arrestox B. Typesetting by The Composing Room, Inc., Kimberly, WI.